# Messages of Love and Healing

## Jennie's Gifts Book 1

# Messages of Love and Healing

## Jennie's Gifts Book 1

## LYNN THOMAS

Net Partners Publishing
2012 USA

# Copyright

*Messages of Love and Healing*
*Jennie's Gifts Book 1*

Copyright ©2012 Lynn Seeley Thomas,
Updated 2013, 2014, 2015
http://lynnthomas.info

All rights reserved. No part of this book may be used,
stored, transmitted or reproduced in any manner
without written permission from the author, except in
brief quotations embodied in reviews and articles.

This is a work of fiction. Names, characters, places and
incidents are either products of the author's imagination
or used fictitiously. Any resemblance to actual persons,
living or dead, business establishments, events or
locales is entirely coincidental. All trademarks and
brand names used in this book are the property of their
respective owners.

Published by NetPartnersPublishing.com
Published in the United States of America
Vsn 2015619

Print ISBN#: 0970241798

# Jennie's Gifts Series

" ... a feel-good read in and of itself, but filled with spiritual wisdom that will open your heart and lift your soul. We need more books like Jennie's Gifts and more authors like Lynn Thomas." ~ Suzanne Giesemann, Hay House author of "Messages of Hope"

"An inspiring novel about a medium's experiences that both teaches and entertains while allowing the reader to see into the world of spirit communication." ~ Elizabeth Owens, author of "Discover Your Spiritual Life"

"Jennies Gifts was given to me by a friend after the loss of my young daughter. It was so comforting; I couldn't stop reading it until I had completed the entire book. It helped heal my heart and lifted my spiritual needs as well as the educational value received. I will be giving this book as gifts many times, and awaiting the next book by Lynn Thomas." ~ Kathy Kelly

"Wow I loved the book!!!! Being a medium reading this book was awesome because you can relate to so many of the sessions that Jennie did and all she experienced. Great explanations of how one sees spirit and gives the message. Jennie's family dynamic was REAL! So when is the next book?" ~ Joan Piper, mediumship instructor

"I finished your book and it was fantastic... with an ending that I didn't expect. Really good!" ~ Brenda Ingle

"...I needed this book... was great timing. This Jennie's journey is kind of my journey as well... this book was very inspiring... Thank you."~ Yukari

"...a lovely story of personal growth. The author did a great job explaining the life of a medium, and I came away having learned something. The book was an easy read, very enjoyable and recommended..." JT

# Acknowledgements

My loving gratitude to my husband, my family and my friends for their loving encouragement. Specific thanks to Mary "Tish" Ebling for editing this book and to Angela P. Thomas in the creation of the original cover design. Heartfelt thanks to medium, Joan Piper, for her instruction, guidance and inspiration; and to all of my wonderful mentors and peers. Grateful thanks to authors Suzanne Giesemann and Elizabeth Owens for their book reviews. Many thanks to Rev. Catherine Ponder and to all who serve to enlighten and empower us on our path. And a special thanks to the creative and loving Spirit that resides in all of us.

# Dedication

*To my husband Tom Thomas,*
*Thank you for encouraging me.*

*And to my mentor Joan Piper,*
*Thank you for "stretching" me.*

# CHAPTER ONE

## *September*

I STOOD ON the sidewalk outside my newly rented store, gazing up at the new Sunflowers Shoppe sign above the front door. A smaller sign that hung beneath it said, Jennifer Malone, Medium. And the sign-painter had added sunflowers to both signs and the front windows.

The reason I had named my store Sunflowers was because the sunflower is the symbol of mediumship. It's said that the sunflower turns its face to the sun, like spiritual beings turn their face to the light of God. The sunflower will seek out the light, no matter how little light there is. This represents having faith and belief in things unseen. And the sunflower is a symbol of good luck, something I needed for my new venture.

As I admired my new signage this September evening, I stood in a place I had glimpsed throughout my life, but had rarely given serious thought to until recently. I was at last announcing to the world, well at least to the small town of Del Vista, Florida, that I was a medium and now openly living my purpose.

And once I made that decision, all the pieces, including this great location, had fallen into place. It was as Ralph Waldo Emerson had stated, 'Once you make a decision, the universe conspires to make it happen'. It felt good to have finally stepped onto my spiritual path. I felt certain that this was what I was born to do, and this shop would serve that purpose.

From the storefront windows I could see the shelves and tables filled with crystals, books and other items for sale. Off to one side was a waiting area and a space for giving lectures. At the back of the store was a long hallway that led to two offices for private readings. And at the end of the hallway was my apartment. I didn't have to commute; I could simply walk home.

And with the store located just off the main town square, it was visible and convenient, yet secluded enough for anyone not wanting to be seen going to a medium. Yes, it was perfect, and it had all come together quite nicely.

As I stood on the sidewalk admiring the store, the wind picked up and blew my hair out of place. As I tucked the stray strands behind my ear, I noticed an elderly man standing next to me, looking up at the signs.

I was about to say something to him when he said, "Bah. Medium, psychic, crapola."

I turned toward him. "Pardon me?"

"She must not be any good," he said, then leaned over and spat into one of my newly potted geraniums.

I cringed as I looked at the plant, then back at him and asked, "Why did you say she's no good?"

"Because if she was any good she'd know we don't want that," he said, pointing toward my sign for emphasis, "in our town."

"We don't want what?"

"That," he said pointing more emphatically at the sign. "We don't want con artists here."

"Con artists?" What was this man babbling about? I looked around to see if anyone else was within earshot of our conversation, but saw we were alone.

"Yeah, nothing but conniving, no good pranksters with their bag of tricks," he said, then shoved his hands into his pockets, and kicked at a stone.

"Why are you so upset?" I asked him.

"Because they are all rip-off artists," he said and folded his arms tight across his chest.

"Why do you say that?"

"Not one of them is any damn good," he said shaking his head. "Not one of them is able to talk to my Myrtle, God rest her soul. They just take my money and scam me."

He looked at me now, and for the first time I saw the emotional pain in his eyes. His eyes misted and he wiped away the tears with his hand. "My Myrtle's been gone three years now, and I know that she loved me," he said as his face reddened in anger. "She loved me I tell ya, and if it's possible for anyone to get a message to someone after they are dead, my Myrtle would have done so."

"I'm sorry to hear of your loss," I said.

"Thank you," he said.

I extended my hand toward him. "My name is Jennie. Jennie Malone."

He unfolded his arms and shook my hand, then glanced up at the sign and blushed as recognition registered on his face. He released my hand, nodded toward the sign and said, "That's you? You're her?"

"Yes, that's me," I said. "And you are?"

"My name is Carl. Carl Bertrand. And my wife was Myrtle," he said as he looked down at his shoes, then glanced back at me. "We would have celebrated our fiftieth anniversary this year."

"Would you like to come in, Carl?" I asked as I pointed at the front door.

He looked surprised. "Go in there? With you? Why?"

I walked toward the door, then turned and looked at him. It was getting dark, and the wind had increased. "Come on in, Carl," I said with a nod toward the front entry.

"Well, I don't know."

"No charge, Carl, this one's on me," I said. As I turned the knob and opened the door, the wind chimes rang out from where they hung over the doorframe. The wooden floor creaked beneath my steps as I walked across the room and switched on a lamp.

I glanced back at Carl. I won't stay in business long if I give free readings, but I felt that with Carl I'd make an exception. And Carl's reading would serve to test my newly proven skills. I had to now trust what I had learned. Carl needed help, and I hoped to offer it, even if at the moment he was not a willing participant.

Carl stood in the threshold of the doorway, looking uncertain. His hands were dug deep into the pockets. His head hung down, his shoulders slumped. It was obvious from his stance that he was debating his next move. I sensed that he could not bear another disappointment at not receiving a message from his wife.

As I watched Carl, a presence entered the room. I felt certain it was his beloved Myrtle.

*'How can I get him to sit down with me? How can I help him relax?'* I telepathically asked the spirit.

"Offer him a cup of hot tea," Myrtle said.

"Would you like a hot cup of tea, Carl?" I asked him.

He looked up at me. "What kind?"

"We have black pekoe or green tea and an assortment of herbal teas."

"I'll have the black tea," he said as he entered the room and shut the front door to the cooling night air. He removed his hat and twirled it in his hands as he walked toward me in the waiting area.

I stood at the coffee counter and placed a tea bag in a cup, then added hot water. "Sugar? Milk? Honey?"

"No, that's fine," he said as he took the warm cup from my hands. "Thank you," he said offering me his first smile.

I poured myself a cup of tea, then walked over to one of the chairs and motioned for Carl to join me. He sat in a chair opposite mine and placed his hat on his knee. We both sipped at our tea a moment, then placed our cups on the coffee table.

My arms tingled with energy as Myrtle's presence grew stronger. I began to feel excited as I picked up on her joy at having the opportunity to get a message to her husband.

"Let's just see how this goes, Carl," I said. "Is that okay with you?"

Carl nodded.

# CHAPTER TWO

I CLOSED MY eyes, said a prayer, then silently connected with the spirit realm. I opened my eyes and looked at a scene unfolding next to Carl. I described what I was seeing, which was similar to describing each scene as a movie played.

"I see a gazebo. It's in a park," I said. "There is snow on the ground and behind the gazebo is a pond. There are ice skaters on the pond. In the gazebo is a woman, and she is the one who is bringing me to this scene. She is wearing a full length white winter coat, black gloves and her white hat is trimmed with a black band holding a gray feather."

"Myrtle had a hat like that," Carl said excitedly. "How do you know that?"

Without commenting, I held to the vision and continued my narrative. "The woman is checking her watch. She is waiting for someone who is late. But she waits patiently as she watches the ice skaters. Someone approaches her. She stands to greet him. This is the person she was waiting for. She is now showing me a diamond ring. It's an engagement ring."

"That's where I proposed to her. We were at the gazebo," Carl said. "I had to work late, and was afraid she wouldn't be there. But she had waited for me."

I listened to the spirit, then repeated, "She says it's the most beautiful ring she had ever seen."

Carl wiped at the tears in his eyes. "That's what she said when I gave it to her. I always hoped she meant it. It was all I could afford at the time."

I looked at him. "Yes, she meant it. That's why she wore it all her life."

Carl nodded. "She never wanted another one, even when I could afford better."

My attention returned to the vision. "Now she is standing in a room holding a baby. On the wall are four framed photos of her children, but the baby she is holding is not in any of them." I silently asked the spirit what this meant, and learned it was a new symbol. "Did she lose a baby, Carl?"

He looked at me, his face flushed. "Yes, she lost the last one in childbirth. We had four boys. She lost the girl. We never had anymore."

The spirit of the baby aged and stood next to her mother, holding her hand. Then, both the mother and her child stepped out of the movie and stood next to Carl, looking at him.

The child let go of her mother's hand and hugged her father. I said, "Your wife is with your daughter. They are both happy to see you, and the child is hugging you."

Carl took a handkerchief from his pocket and wiped his eyes, then looked hard at me and asked, "Is this some kind of trick?"

His comment surprised me. "No, Carl, I promise you, no tricks. I'm telling you what I am seeing; what your wife is showing me."

He sat quietly as I silently asked Myrtle, *'Give me more evidence.'* I heard a song, and said, "I hear a voice singing, 'All The Way'."

"That's one of Myrtle's favorite songs. How do you know that?"

"I don't know it, Myrtle does."

Now that I had delivered evidence to Carl that this was Myrtle, I listened for her message. She said, "Tell him I'm okay and I'm waiting for him."

I repeated this to Carl, but he didn't respond as he sat silent in his thoughts.

Myrtle said, "Tell him to call Jerry. It's not right for them to not speak."

"Carl," I said. He looked at me. "Myrtle is saying that you need to call Jerry. She says that it's not right for you to not speak."

"She's talking about our eldest boy," he said with a look of surprise. "I can't even remember what we got mad about. I guess I keep waiting on Jerry to call me."

"She wants you to call him, Carl. She says it's been long enough, and it's time to mend fences."

"Guess that won't hurt none," he said with a shrug. "What else does she say?" he asked with renewed interest.

I asked Myrtle for more evidence, and she showed me a pasture. There were horses, and I described to Carl all I saw.

"That's my boyhood home! I grew up on a farm in Kentucky. I loved that place and I miss it sometimes. Things seemed so much simpler then," he said with a sigh.

Myrtle brought forth a young girl with braided red hair and a young boy with jet black hair. Both children were wearing overalls.

I told Carl, and he said, "That would be my younger sister and brother. They both died young, in a farming accident."

"Myrtle says they are okay. They are happy and they will also greet you when your time comes."

He sat twirling his hat in his hands.

Myrtle said, "Tell him not to be afraid. He will be okay."

"I've been afraid of dying," he said before I spoke. "It's getting close, I can somehow sense it. When I didn't hear from Myrtle, I figured that once I'm dead that'll be it. But if what you are telling me is true, it means that after death I will be with her."

"I'm not saying your time is up, Carl," I said quickly, "but Myrtle says to not worry about it. When your time comes, you won't be alone. You'll be okay."

"I understand," he said, "and now I can stop fearing it. Thank you for that."

Myrtle nodded and smiled at me, then she and the scenes faded away, a sign that the spirit's message had been delivered.

I looked at my watch, surprised to see thirty minutes had passed since we first sat down together. When I'm in contact with the spirits in this way, I tend to lose all sense of space and time.

"Myrtle's gone, Carl," I said, "I mean, I don't sense her with us now."

"It's okay. I understand what you meant. And thank you, Miss Jennie. You've taken a load off my mind," he said as he rose from the chair. "Now, what do I owe you?" he asked as he reached in his back pocket and pulled out his wallet.

I held up my hand and said, "You don't owe me anything. Like I said before, Carl, this one's on the house."

"Okay. Well, thank you again, Miss Jennie. Good luck to you and your store," he said. He tucked his wallet back in his pocket, placed his cap on his head, and walked out the door.

I thanked the spirits, my guides and my higher self for assisting me in my service. I was happy to have helped Myrtle deliver her message to Carl, and felt honored to have been part of the process.

I locked the front door, then walked over to close the window blinds. But first, I glanced outside. The streetlights had come on, and I could see Carl walking away down the dimly lit sidewalk. Where was he going? What was he thinking? I hoped he felt at peace. I hoped I had helped him.

I felt my own sense of inner peace at having come full circle, back into the understanding I had intuited as a child. In using my Gifts I am happy to be of service in helping spirits deliver their messages of love and healing.

# CHAPTER THREE

AS A CHILD, I sensed the oneness state of the Source essence in and around me. I saw the pulsating colorful energy vibrations and auras, and heard the whispering of angels and guides. I could communicate with loved ones who had passed over. And I understood that we were all spiritual beings who had chosen to incarnate on this Earth plane of human experience.

But in the home where I grew up, speaking of such things was not tolerated. And the deceased were not mentioned but on their birthdays, holidays or the anniversary of their passing. Didn't anyone else see Grandpa or the other spirits? And why wasn't I allowed to talk about the spirit world?

Over the years I'd dabble at times in the etheric, but with each passing year my sense of knowing faded more. Like a pendulum, I had swung from the metaphysical into the third dimensional world. Yet I always felt some longing to return to the spiritual side.

A few years ago, the pendulum swung back, and I was fortunate to find a knowledgeable teacher. Sara Kelsey's mediumship instruction helped me realize that the spirit world was real and has much to tell us about this life. The spirits are happy to be of service and stand at hand, ready to offer guidance. I am happy to now be of service to the spirit realms, and enjoy the communication. And Sara's training is what activated the path that led to the opening of my store.

As I looked out the window, leaves were blowing along the street. Autumn was at our doorstep, and we were in for a cool night. I closed the front curtains, and walked over to the gas fireplace and lit it. I sat back in my chair, sipping my now cooled cup of tea. As I watched the flames lick at the logs, I recalled the dream that had inspired me to become a professional medium.

In the dream, my mother had taken me by the hand to see my father. "Your daughter has something to tell you," she said, which was reminiscent of my childhood. When I had done or said something I shouldn't have, my mother would take me by the hand to tell my father about it. As a child, it was always a challenging confrontation, and in the dream I felt that same trepidation.

My father was sitting in a chair and I took a seat facing him. He looked at me as my mother walked away, barely in view, which was also what she would do.

"I have something important to tell you, Dad, and I need you to hear me out," I said.

He nodded and waited for me to begin.

"I've seen spirits since I was a child; mostly Grandpa, but there were others."

This seemed to pique his interest as he raised an eyebrow.

I told him I had talked with spirits, and some would sit with me while I played with my dolls. I told him that when I started going to school Mom told me to stop talking about such things.

He seemed surprised to learn of this.

Then I told him how after all these years I could still hear and see spirits. And I told him I was taking mediumship classes. "I can easily communicate with spirits in class," I said. "But I'm not certain I can elsewhere." I pondered this a moment, then added, "Perhaps it's the group setting or that I can connect better when I'm with my instructor."

He nodded, and leaned toward me, showing interest.

"I enjoy the classes, and find it interesting and rewarding. But I've never used my spiritual Gifts as my life's work. I've always sought income elsewhere."

I waited while he thought about all I had told him.

He smiled and said, "I think it would make a great career."

I was stunned. I never expected such a reply from my father, not even in a dream. And it occurred to me, I had sought his permission my whole life!

I awoke remembering the dream and it stayed with me. It felt like I had actually spoken with my father. And I laughed when it dawned on me that I had tried to convince my deceased father I could communicate with spirits. That dream, and his permission, changed my life. I had received the go ahead to live my passion.

It was after that I completed my training and opened my Sunflowers Shoppe. I plan to offer not only readings, but classes, workshops and lectures. This place will serve those plans quite well.

I walked over and turned off the fireplace, then stood listening to the wind howling through the trees. I walked through the storefront, turning off all but the night lights as I made my way down the hall. When I entered my apartment I said aloud to no one, "I'm home."

As I closed the door I felt a pang of loneliness. While I had focused on getting my life on track, I longed to have someone to share it. A close companion with a knowing smile, a gentle touch, and a warm caress. Someone not at all like Ben.

Divorcing him had turned out to be a blessing. He would have never agreed to my being a medium. With Ben, the focus was always on him, his talents and pursuits. He never encouraged mine. He never would have honored or approved of my gifts.

And our daughter, Kate, was being as insensitive as her father. She had renounced my Gifts and that I was a medium. "You're doing what?" she had said. "Are you kidding me? What will people think?"

Her words had stung. And the more I tried to convince her that this was a sane, rational and practical business for me to open, the harder she protested. Why did Kate think she knew better what was best for me? What will it take for her to accept and support my new career?

Even if she didn't agree with me, why couldn't she offer her loving support? Like when I've told her, or her brother, at times, 'I don't agree with your choice or your behavior, but I love you. I'm here for you'. Why couldn't she offer that to me?

The worst part was that I wasn't allowed to share my views or experiences with my grandchildren. I had to be on my guard, and unable to be myself around them. And worse, Kate refused to let them even come to my apartment.

"If you want to see Evan and Lola," she told me last month during a phone conversation, "you will have to come here. They are not ever going there."

Hadn't I raised Kate better than this? It seemed that she was open-minded about anyone but me.

Her husband, Brad, was at least tolerant of my life choices. Perhaps he'd eventually get Kate to visit me and see the store. It pained my heart that she had refused to do so. I loved her, so I tried to make space for her point of view, even if I didn't like it.

She had been influenced by her father, which was nothing new. She usually sided with him, and saw me as wrong or the bad guy. But I can't wait for Kate or her father, equally appalled and skeptical of my new profession, to catch up. It was each soul's responsibility how it lives its life, and I had to live mine my way, with or without their approval.

Thankfully Kate and my ex-husband lived an hour away, which gave me a sense of space and distance from their criticism, and...

I stopped and let out a sigh. I knew better. When the mind starts complaining, the best thing to do is to stop and say, "That's not what I want to think about. Now, what do I want to think about?"

[12]

Nathan. Per usual, our son supported me one hundred percent. "Go for it Mom, make me proud," he said when I told him my news. I wished he lived closer instead of sixteen hours away in Portage Lakes, Ohio. I missed him, his wife and daughter terribly. But even at that distance, Nathan's support helped fuel my confidence in going forward.

My son was more like me in personality; but braver. If he had experienced these Gifts the way I always have, he would not have taken this long to live them. And he is so supportive of my doing what has taken me till the age of fifty to finally embrace. His daughter, Emily, is lucky to have chosen him as her father. With his loving support behind her, who knows what she'll achieve. Nathan was certainly a blessing in my life.

I strive to end each day being grateful and counting my blessings before bed. So I stood at the bathroom mirror, gazed into my eyes and affirmed aloud, "I desire peace in my family, loving each other without judgment. I desire peace with my ex-husband." That one was still hard to say.

"I desire a loving relationship with a steady, reliable, strong, loving, vibrant, wise, healthy and handsome man. I desire that my Sunflowers Shoppe is a success. I am ready to be of service to my clients and to spirit. And I desire to be safe in my new home and have a good night's sleep. May God bless me, my family and the world. So be it. Amen."

I walked into the bedroom, kicked off my slippers, slipped off my robe and tossed it on the rocking chair. I had bought that bedside chair for reading. But each night I was too tired from painting walls, scrubbing floors, and stacking inventory. There had been more to do than I first realized. And so, as much as I'd enjoy reading Evanovich's newest *Stephanie Plum* novel, it would have to wait.

I slid into bed, and turned off the light. In the darkness, there were lots of strange noises that amplified at night when sleeping in a new place. That sound must be the water in the pipes. That noise must be the furnace coming on. My mind was on alert and my eyes wide open as I peeked out from the covers.

I may need to get a dog.

# CHAPTER FOUR

THE NEXT MORNING, I awoke and leisurely stretched and yawned, until I realized what day it was. The Sunflowers Shoppe officially opens for business today! It was the first day of a new beginning.

I jumped out of bed, pulled on my robe and sat in my rocking chair to meditate. It was important that I took the time to connect with my intuition. As I took slow, rhythmic breaths I released the mental chatter, which soon gave way to a state of bliss. I ended my meditation with a declaration for clear guidance throughout my day.

For breakfast I made a slice of toasted bread slathered with almond butter and fresh pineapple slices. As I ate, I performed a mental tally of the store's new inventory of books, cards, posters, incense, oils, candles, and candle holders. I purchased one of the whimsical cat votive holders for my living room as I so enjoyed how the candlelight animated the cat's face. I had also inventoried music and videos, wall hangings, window decals, banners and wind chimes. And I had stocked the front glass display cases with jewelry, crystals and wands. The opening of

Sunflowers had kept me busy, and I was happy with all my decisions, especially in hiring Megan.

I had needed someone to be both my assistant and manage the storefront while I focused on readings. I placed a help-wanted sign in the front window and posted an ad online. I interviewed several men and women, but when Megan walked in, I knew she was the one. She exuded a youthful vitality, and was so outgoing and friendly I liked her right away.

But I was a bit concerned that she could only work part time until January. She was in college and when her schedule changed in the new semester, she would work full time. I wanted to give her the chance. as I felt a connection with her. She reminded me of myself at her age; enthusiastic and full of creative ideas. It was her joyfully radiant personality that decided it, as I was certain she would help my customers feel welcomed.

I went to the closet and pulled my long green and blue striped dress from its hanger. After dressing, I brushed my shoulder length blonde hair, noticing a few gray hairs appearing. I had stopped wearing mascara months ago as it tends to irritate my eyes. But I still slather on foundation in the hope of smoothing out and hiding any wrinkles. I looked in the mirror to check my appearance, then affirmed, "Today is a great day."

I walked over to the door and opened it. There before me stood Sunflowers, my dream a reality. I felt excited and grateful for this new venture. I closed the apartment door, walked down the hallway to the storefront and flipped on all the lights. I opened the blinds at the front windows and looked out at the clear blue sky and the sunshine. What a beautiful day! I unlocked the front door and flipped the open sign to face the street. The Sunflowers Shoppe was open for business.

In the waiting area, I turned on the single-serve coffee maker so the water would be hot and ready for clients and shoppers desiring a cup of freshly brewed coffee or tea. As I placed a tea bag in my mug, the wind chimes rang out above the front door. It was Deanna.

My friend was a few years older than me and had embraced her silver hair, wearing it cropped short which accentuated her hazel eyes. She smiled at me and said, "Good morning" as she closed the door behind her.

"Good morning," I said. "Are you ready for our new adventure?"

"I guess so," she said. Her smile faded into a frown, as she nervously tugged at her sweater.

"What's wrong?"

"I hope I'm ready for this."

"What do you mean?"

"It's just that I haven't given a message for a while now. What if I've lost my touch?"

"Stop worrying, you'll do fine."

Deanna and I had met at Sara Kelsey's mediumship training. When I decided to open Sunflowers I offered her one of my two offices. She had agreed to sublet the space in the hopes of also starting her own business. And she had liked the idea of us working together. But as opening day neared, Deanna grew doubtful and insecure.

"Do you have any appointments today?"

"Yes, I met someone in the health food store the other day. We got to talking, and I handed her my business card. She phoned me yesterday and made an appointment for this morning."

"That's great," I said.

"Yeah, great," she said with feigned enthusiasm.

"Well, your office awaits you," I said with a smile as I pointed toward the hallway. "Why don't you get settled in before she arrives?"

"Good idea," Deanna said as she flung her car keys into her tote bag and walked toward her office.

The door chimes rang again. It was Megan, dressed in a sweater and jeans, her black hair pulled back in a tight ponytail. She was carrying her purse and books.

"Good morning, Megan," I said.

"Good morning, Jennie," Megan said as she walked behind the counter and stowed her things.

"Do you need me to go over anything with you?"

"No, I think I got it," she said as she switched on the cash register and lit the glass display case under the front counter.

When we had gone over everything the other day she impressed with her sharp focus. I wished Deanna had the same confidence and enthusiasm.

"Okay," I said, "just ask if you have any questions, unless I'm in a reading, of course."

"Yes, I remember."

I glanced out the front window and saw that the trees were already changing color. Autumn had always been my favorite time of year, with the drier and cooler air. Mother Nature's fall palette was colorful even in Central Florida. "I wonder what the day will bring."

I walked to my office and stood in the doorway enjoying the view. I enjoyed the look and feel of my new work space. Along the far wall was an antique-looking roll top desk that when closed hid my laptop and paperwork. My desk chair swiveled from my desk to my reading table. The table provided a useful surface for taking notes or working with crystals or other items during a reading. Two upholstered chairs on the opposite side of the table provided seating for my clients. Behind the chairs and along the opposite wall was a sofa and two end tables.

# CHAPTER FIVE

I SAT AT my roll top desk and opened the laptop. I clicked on my journal file and began my morning ritual of typing at least three pages of whatever was on my mind. I referred to this as my *mind dump*, where I release and sweep away pesky thoughts, worries and concerns. This was similar to t h e *Morning Pages* technique written about in Julia Cameron's book, *The Artist's Way*. Doing this daily helps me to create space above the mind chatter.

I was about ten minutes into my journal when I sensed someone behind me. I turned around and saw Megan standing in my doorway.

"Someone is here for a reading," she said.

"I don't recall having any appointments this morning."

"He doesn't have one. He walked in and asked to see you," she said.

We walked to the end of the hall, then stopped to peek at the storefront. "Do you mean him?" I asked as I pointed at a young man standing at the coffee counter.

"Yes," Megan said.

"He looks young," I said. "Didn't we discuss this? Anyone under eighteen needs a parent or adult's permission, even if they don't sit with them for the reading."

"Yes, you told me, but he says he's twenty-one," she whispered. "He told me that everyone thinks he's younger than he is."

"Did you ask to see his ID?"

Megan blushed. "No."

"Why not?"

"It's embarrassing. He's my age."

I sighed. "Look, here's what you do. Go out there and tell him that your manager said that he needs to either show you his ID or bring an adult back with him."

"Do I have to?" she asked with pleading eyes.

"Yes, you have to," I said and gave her a gentle shove toward the storefront. I stayed back and watched Megan approach the young man. He looked annoyed by what she was saying. But if he's really twenty-one, he'll show his ID, otherwise... yup, there he goes out the door.

Megan turned to look at me and shrugged. I had to laugh, but hey, she followed through. She'd do all right as my store manager.

A loud sigh came from Deanna's office. I knocked on her door and said, "Are you okay?"

"Come in," she said.

I stepped into her office and saw her sitting slumped down in her chair.

"What's wrong? Why the big sigh?" I asked.

"I'm so nervous about giving a reading that I'm freaking myself out," she said.

"Stage jitters, huh?"

She laughed. "You could call it that."

"Let me tell you something," I said as I sat across from her. "I gave a reading here last night."

This caught her interest, and she sat up and leaned toward me. "You did? Tell me about it."

"His name was Carl Bertrand," I said, and gave her the details. I told her how reluctant he had been, and how Myrtle helped me give the evidential and deliver her message to him. "It was just like in Sara's class. I gave the evidence, then I gave the message. Spirit works with us here, too," I said, tapping her desk for emphasis. "Not only did Carl seem happier when he left, but I felt better, too."

"Wow, that's great! But why didn't you charge him a fee?"

I shrugged. "It was a combination of things, but mostly an impulsive decision. He had been disappointed before, and I doubt he would have sat with me had I charged him. Besides, he was here for more than a message from his dear departed wife."

"What do you mean?"

"It proved I could give messages beyond the classroom, and it reminded me that this work is not about us; it's about the message."

"I see what you mean," Deanna said, "but I fear it was Sara who made my abilities possible. It came so easy in her classroom."

"No, I think Sara's classes helped make it easier to believe because we were part of a focused group. But the essence of spirit is wherever we are. Spirit's not waiting to work with us in some classroom, but here, too. We have to allow the connection and too much thinking, fear or doubt blocks our connection no matter where we are."

Deanna sighed and said, "You could be right. Hey, do you remember our first reading together?"

"How could I forget? You were so condescending."

"I was? What do you mean?"

"Don't you remember? When Sara paired us off at that initial workshop, you told me more than once that you had been to Sara's classes before. You assumed you knew more than me without knowing anything about me."

"That wasn't about you. It was more an affirmation. You know, like, 'I've done this before and I'll do it again.'"

"Oh? Why? Were you nervous?"

"I feared my success in her other classes had been a fluke. I felt like a fraud and doubted I could give more readings."

I laughed. "And here you are worried again. Do you really think your Gifts turn off? Is that it? Let me ask you, have you ever had a hunch about something?"

"You mean intuition? Of course, I've had hunches my whole life."

"Did it matter where you were?"

"No, of course not."

"So why do you think your connection to spirit is only possible in the classroom?"

"It does sound ridiculous when you say it out loud."

"Most fears are ridiculous when held to the light," I said. "Just remember your training. Step into the spirit and give what you get. And remember, it's not about us, and it's not up to us, so don't worry and you'll do fine."

"Thanks for the pep talk, Jennie."

I stood from the chair and said, "Just relax and have fun." As I turned to leave, I glanced back and saw that she had closed her eyes for meditation.

Whatever else the day brings, I'm happy my friend was here to share it.

# CHAPTER SIX

I SAT TYPING at my computer when Megan rushed up to my desk. "What's up?" I asked.

"A man came in the store asking for a reading."

"Well, that's what we do," I said.

"But he's so handsome," she said fanning her face, acting faint.

"Well, we serve all kinds," I said with a laugh and followed her to the waiting area. My first glance at the fine specimen of man seated there impressed me too. I looked at his full head of gray and brown hair. Why is it men can wear gray so well? And he had laugh lines around his eyes and at his mouth. He must smile a lot, then he smiled at me!

He stood to greet me and I was drawn in by his deep blue eyes. He was a few inches taller than me, and had such a rugged physique, he must keep active. He wore a blue and white checkered shirt tucked into the belted waist line of his form fitting jeans. A handsome man indeed. I blushed.

Whoa, girl, act professional! I forced my feet into the floor to steady myself and said, "I'm Jennie. Would you like a reading?"

"Yes, I would, Jennie," he said. "I'm Jake Walker."

Was that a twinkle in his eye? An electric spark ran up my arms as we shook hands. This man was magnetic, and

I felt stirrings I hadn't had in years, if ever. I was drawn to this guy. I liked him and he felt familiar, but I couldn't place him.

I smiled at him and said, "It's a pleasure to meet you, Jake, come with me." I led him to my office and ushered him to one of the chairs. I took a seat opposite him at the reading table and opened my notebook to a fresh page. As I wrote the date and his name at the top, I said, "How did you find us?"

"I drove by yesterday, saw the new signs, and decided to give this a try. I've never been to a psychic before, but I'm searching for an answer."

"I see, but, I'm not a psychic, I'm a medium."

"What's the difference?"

"A psychic reads or senses the subtle energies around you. A medium rises up in vibration and connects with spirit. Not all psychics are mediums, but all mediums are psychic."

"Oh."

"Do you work in town?"

"Yes, I work at the Del Vista Golf Shop."

"Oh I've seen the carts on display there. Some look quite amusing."

"Yes, the ones resembling miniature cars are popular."

"Do you sell many of them?"

"Oh yes, mostly the custom ones as the folks at the country club like outdoing each other," he said with a laugh.

His laugh lines creased when he smiled. My goodness he was handsome. "So you design golf carts?" I asked.

"No, I manage the pro shop, though I'd rather golf. I guess you could call me a bit of a golf nut," he said.

"Are you a golf pro?"

"I wish. No, I'm far from being a pro. I didn't take up the game till I was in my forties, but since working at the pro shop, I've a deeper interest in the game. If I had known when I was younger that one could have a career playing golf, I might have pursued it, but I'm not sure I would have been good enough. The more I golf, the more I respect what the pros can do. Do you golf?"

"I golfed many years ago with my husband," I said.

"Well, anytime you'd like to start again, I can help you and your husband get fitted with the proper gear."

He thought I was still married. Maybe that's just as well. I needed to be professional, and sat up taller in my chair. "Thanks for the offer, Jake. Now, let's focus on why you are here today."

"Sounds good," Jake said with a smile. "I need to make some decisions. I'm hoping you can give me the answers. I'd like to know if..."

"Wait," I said as I held up my hand, "I'd rather you didn't tell me too much. Let's see what message spirit has for you, okay?"

"Okay," he said with a shrug. "I just hope I get my answer."

"Give me a minute," I said, and closed my eyes to plug into spirit. There was a strong presence near. When I opened my eyes, there was a spirit who looked like a Native American Chief. He wore a long feathered headdress, exuded power and I sensed he had great knowledge. I described him to Jake.

"Cool," he said.

I listened to the Chief and said, "His name is Red Hawk. He says he was with you at the golf course yesterday."

"I did notice a hawk while golfing yesterday."

"He says, when you get a great golf shot, when you connect perfectly with the ball, it's a feeling of relief. The focused desire to reach the green before you hit the ball, is what lets you hit it perfectly. It's an intention of focused energy. He says it's all about energy. He says that is why you like being near waterfalls; it's the ions. Whether at golf or at the waterfalls, you thrive in that energy."

"I do enjoy sitting by a waterfall," Jake said.

I held to the Chief's vision. "He says, it's easier to hit a green that you can see, but pros can land on a green too far away to see. They envision it in their mind as they swing the club. Envision your life desires as if you are envisioning hitting the green. Lift up your energy for a sense of relief. Focus on the feeling first, in whatever you do."

"Okay," Jake said.

A woman in spirit appeared next to the Chief. She held up her left hand to show me her wedding ring. I heard the name Connie, and told Jake.

Jake's eyes misted. "Connie was my wife's name."

I felt a tug at my heart as I sensed how deeply he loved and missed her, and a twinge of guilt at lusting over him in her presence. "She stands next to you and says she is okay."

"How does she look?" he asked.

I described her to him. "She has long auburn hair and is wearing a flowing dress. She looks radiant and is smiling at you."

"That's a relief," he said. "She battled the cancer a long time."

Connie said, "Tell him I'm happy he's found golf. Keep doing the things you enjoy."

I relayed her message, and added, "She wants you to be happy."

He nodded and said, "I've missed her." And the sadness on his face reflected what he felt in his heart.

# CHAPTER SEVEN

CONNIE FADED FROM view, but the Chief was still with us.

Jake asked, "Why am I having this pain in my neck?"

The Chief responded, and I repeated, "You are pushing, straining, and striving. The pain comes from the emotional and the mental bodies pressing down on the physical one."

The Chief held out his hand to show a hawk, then the hawk flew into the air. The Chief pointed toward the sky, and I described it all to Jake, then said, "His message is to lift up, rise up, ease up into relief. Elevate your thoughts by being more in the now moment. Stop straining about your future."

Spirit hands appeared at Jake's neck, rubbing him and I nearly swooned. "Massage could be helpful. I have oils in the store," I said as I toyed with the idea of massaging his neck. An image of Connie came to mind, and I plugged back into the spiritual stream.

"The Chief is showing me a forest with several pathways. This symbolizes choice. Each pathway or choice can split into more paths. There is no should; you determine your path. Whatever you decide will be okay if you first pay attention to how you feel before making a decision. This is most important. Does a choice feel like relief?"

The Chief showed me a hawk flying over the forest from the hawk's point of view. There was a rabbit on the forest floor, too low to the ground to see the different pathways.

I described this to Jake, and said, "The rabbit symbolizes your lower thoughts or energies. The hawk symbolizes your higher mind and energies. Lift up your energy. Tap into your higher level of thought. Know you are the master of the forest. Decide the path by the feeling. This will serve you. And he suggests that you meditate to receive guidance and answers. You can't get the answers you seek unless you connect with your higher self, your higher mind. Again, it's that elevated feeling and mentality that offers clarity."

Jake sighed and said, "I wish he'd just give me my answer."

The Chief looked at Jake, and said, "Tell him I am here to guide him, not to tell him what to do. He has to make his own decisions, but I can help raise his energy."

I relayed this to Jake who did not look happy with the message.

The Chief said, and I repeated, "This is your life quest. You desired to come into this incarnation. He is one of your guides. Understand that you are master of your quest. You can get your own answers."

A vision of a young man entered the forest wearing a cloak. The hawk flew down and lifted away the cloak. The young man stood tall, dressed as a warrior and raised his arms. I described this to Jake, and said, "You have been thinking like a victim, but you are the master, the warrior of your life."

The Chief again showed me the forest from above. I described this and repeated, "Rise up to see the paths from a higher place. Determine what feels right. Also notice the signs. What glistens or shines? There are breadcrumbs all around you."

The Chief said, "Tell him it's about the feeling. Follow the feeling to the answers."

I repeated what he said, and added, "Call on Red Hawk when you meditate and he will help you lift up. He is here to help you. He says you have helped each other over many lifetimes. You are like brothers and he loves you, so call on him."

"He's my brother?" Jake said.

Out of the whole message, that was the only comment Jake latched onto? "He is referring to being with you over many lifetimes."

"But he's a Chief."

"That is the way he is presenting himself for this reading. He could have dressed another way, but this served as the best personification for this message. That's what spirits do."

"Huh," Jake said.

The Chief smiled at me and faded away. Red Hawk's message had been helpful for not only the recipient, known as the *sitter,* but for me as well. Red Hawk reminded me to meditate more, and to follow my feelings to desired good. I thanked Red Hawk and my guides for their assistance, then remembered the oil.

"Do you want the massage oil?"

"I guess so, but first I want to ask you something."

"What is it?"

"How do you do that?"

"How do I do what?" I asked as I stood from my chair.

"How do you know what they are saying? How do you see them?"

"It's kind of like watching a movie while describing what I am hearing and seeing to you."

"Huh," Jake said.

# CHAPTER EIGHT

## *Week Two*

OUR FIRST WEEK of business had gone well. Deanna and I had read for several clients and Megan was selling out of items in the storefront. Word of mouth had quickly spread about Sunflowers. Megan came to my doorway. "What's up?"

"He's back," Megan said.

"Who's back?"

"That guy who was here last week. The one you said to ask for his ID. Remember?"

"Oh, yeah. He is?"

"Yes, and he showed me his driver's license. He is twenty-one."

"Why didn't he show it to you then?"

"He said that he was mad that we asked for it. He said that he wasn't sure he even wanted a reading."

"And now?"

"And now he's back and does want a reading."

I laughed. "Well, I'll be free in a few moments," I said, and finished typing a sentence in my journal. I logged off my computer, closed my desk and walked out to the storefront to meet the young man. "Hello, I'm Jennie."

He stood awkwardly, self-consciously, with one hand in the back pocket of his jeans as he said, "Hi. I'm Chad."

"Welcome, Chad. Come with me," I said and led him to my office. I sat in my chair and motioned for him to sit across from me at the table. He sat stiffly and said, "I've never done anything like this before."

"Relax, there's nothing for you to do," I said and closed my eyes to connect with spirit. When I opened my eyes we had company, and I said, "A man is standing behind you. He is perhaps in his sixties with gray hair and beard. He looks strong and has a large frame. He's dressed in mechanic's overalls rolled up at the sleeves. A red handkerchief is hanging from his hip pocket. He is standing next to a tool chest and holding a wrench. He is showing me a muscle car, an old Chevy. He says he liked to work on cars."

"Papaw!" Chad said excitedly. "You are talking about my grandfather. For as long as I can remember he wore overalls like you described, and he worked on his cars. He owned several muscle cars."

The spirit confirmed this by taking one step up behind Chad, my symbol for grandfather. I love how in evidential mediumship the spirits are so wise in how they help the medium let their loved ones know who they are. Papaw smiled at his grandson. "He is happy to be here with you and to have this opportunity to communicate."

Papaw spread out an image of a map and as I looked at it, I soared above it, traveling to the north and east. "He was not from this area," I said and asked for clarification. "He lived in Virginia, near the mountains."

"Yes, that's right," Chad said.

I appreciated his confirmation; so far so good. This was his grandfather, he had lived in Virginia, had dressed as I had described him and he liked working on cars. As the map faded from view I got a strong headache and my vision blurred. This had to have something to do with his passing. And this was the usual sequence of events. First, the spirit appears in a way that is recognizable to the sitter. Next, the spirit shows me how they passed. And then, the jewel of the session... their message of love and healing.

"I'm getting a headache with pain above and behind my eyes," I said. "This has to do with your grandfather's passing."

"He died of an aneurysm," Chad said.

The pain vanished with this acknowledgment, and his grandfather said, "Tell him not to feel guilty."

"Your grandfather says to not feel guilty," I said. "He understands that you could not be with him during his last days, that you were away at college and couldn't get home."

Chad's eyes filled with tears. "I have felt awful about it. Somehow, I got it in my head to go away to college. But I didn't realize until after I moved away how much I'd miss Papaw. We tinkered on the cars together and I loved hearing his jokes and stories. And I missed fishing with him. I missed him so much and didn't realize until I left home that he was the best friend I ever had. And then he died, and it was too late."

Papaw looked at his grandson crying as I repeated what he said. "Your grandfather knows how much you loved him, and that you still do. He loved you very much, and he still does. He says to tell you that he is happy to be free from his painful body. He was sick a long time, but never let on. He didn't want you or your dad or your grandmother to worry. He says to tell you that he is now more alive than ever."

Chad looked surprised. "He's really okay?"

"Yes, he is and he says to call on him and he will come. He looks in on you and the bond you had is still strong. Let go of your guilt and know he loves you dearly."

Chad looked relieved. The heartache he'd been living with seemed to have dissolved. Having delivered the spirit's message, I expected his grandfather to fade from view. But he lingered, there was more he wanted to say.

I listened and said, "Your grandfather says that your family is searching for a document. It's a title or something."

"Yes, that's right," he said.

I saw an old desk and told Chad, "Your grandfather had an old wooden desk." As I watched the scene, the desk drawer came out and there was a document in, no wait, behind it. "Pull the top desk drawer out all the way and you will find the paper stuck behind the drawer."

"I'll tell my dad. He has been looking for the title to one of Papaw's cars. Someone wanted to buy it but Granny couldn't find it."

His grandfather smiled and disappeared; his messages delivered. "Your grandfather has gone, but remember you can call on him and he will visit you."

Chad smiled, and said, "I've felt him near, but thought it was guilt. I debated on coming here the other morning, and when the girl up front asked for my ID, I left. But something pulled me back here, maybe Papaw. I'm glad I came. Thank you."

"You are most welcome. I'm happy to be of service."

As Chad left my office, I thanked my guides for helping me and Papaw help him. My ears picked up as I heard Chad talking at the front counter. He must be talking to Megan. I couldn't hear what they were saying, but I heard her laugh. Was he asking her out? I heard her giggle, then say, "Okay." Could be why he left the other day. He must have felt embarrassed when Megan carded him because he was attracted to her.

# CHAPTER NINE

## *October*

I INTENDED TO record all my readings into my journal. Each one was unique and offered insights from the spirit world. During the past several weeks I've had unusual messages involving a frog, a nature spirit and a wizard.

The frog reading was for a young woman. I had connected with spirit and the first thing I saw was a green frog. At first, it looked live, then like a stuffed toy, and then it transformed into a painting of a frog. This quick transition, from virtual to stuffed to painted, was a bit confusing. I asked the spirit to replay the vision in slow motion. The vision began again, but I couldn't grasp the symbolism, so I simply said, "I see a green frog."

The woman stared at me.

"At first I saw a live frog, then it looked like a stuffed toy. But as quickly as I tell you this, the toy has become a drawing."

She made no comment.

I took a breath and silently asked, '*Who is this?*'

A man appeared behind her chair. "This spirit has dark hair and is quite tall and handsome. He says he is your grandfather. He is again showing me this frog, so it is important."

She nodded.

Why wasn't she saying anything? Why was I seeing this? "Now, he is handing you the toy frog. Did he give you a stuffed toy frog when you were little?"

The woman frowned, then smiled. "Yes, I had forgotten about that."

Now we were getting somewhere. "Do you still have it?"

"I don't, but maybe my mother does. I'll ask her."

"Okay, that's verification. He's showing me a palette of color and drawing paper and the drawing of the frog."

"My grandfather was an artist. He used to let me draw with him."

"Okay, thank you. He is saying that he'd like for you to have that frog, or a similar stuffed frog, at your desk. Each time you look at the frog, you can think of your grandfather and know he is thinking of you. If you can't find the frog he gave you, you will get one some other way. You might see one in a store or someone will give you one soon."

"Okay."

"The reason he is telling us about the frog is because the toy frog on his desk made him laugh. And it reminded him to not take life so seriously. That is why he gave it to you."

"Okay."

"So he asks that you put the frog on your desk. But the painting he shows me is not about him. Are you an artist?"

"I took art in college, but dropped out."

"Painting is a gift you share, and he'd like to paint with you. Place the frog where you paint to remember he is with you. And remember to not take life too seriously."

The woman smiled and said, "Thank you."

☼

The next unusual reading was for an older woman. She came to my office looking quite pensive. As I brought forth the first spirit, it was not a person, but a large blur of green. The green transformed into a beautiful woman wearing a long green dress. Surrounding her and the dress were small pixies and sprites flying in the air. In her hair was a strand of daisies and I got the impression that this was one of the sitter's guides, a nature spirit.

I described what I was getting, and said, "You'd do well at gardening. The earth is grounding for you and balances your energy. You need to get your hands in soil."

"I used to garden, years ago, and I did enjoy it," she said.

"I sense this would be healing on many levels. You would de-stress, feel more balanced and grounded, and receive answers to things that are puzzling you. You have a strong connection to nature, and in nature you can tune in to your intuitive guidance."

The woman laughed and said, "That sounds wonderful."

☼

Another odd reading was for a man. I tuned into a spirit dressed like a wizard. He stood well over seven feet tall, with long black wavy hair, mustache and beard and a long flowing gown. I was so shocked by the vision, I could hardly speak.

When I described the vision, the man said, "Him again?"

"You've heard from him before?"

"Yes, and in my dreams."

The wizard morphed into a clean shaven man wearing a white lab coat and wire-rimmed glasses. He gave me some numbers and equations for the sitter.

I did not understand a word of it. But the sitter was happy to jot the formulas in his notebook, then thanked me.

☼

Besides recording my readings, I am keeping track of insights, new symbols, and other ideas. So far most of my readings have followed a pattern. First an image or vision of the spirit so the sitter can recognize them. A feeling or other sensation about them, their personality or their relationship, how they lived and how they died. But the gem is their message.

My experience has convinced me that spirit is very much alive. While on this planet or plane of existence, we live in individual worlds of thought, perception and emotion. Once deceased, we shed our physical and emotional bodies. We reawaken to ourselves and have knowledge of our incarnations and every lesson learned on each side of the veil. We review our life as our own judge and jury.

And on each side of the veil, we are not alone. Guides and loved ones surround us in their desire to help us become more enlightened to our own being. Connected in the spirit of all that is, we help each other. Spirits try to contact us because they love us, want to help us and they desire to be remembered. This is not something to fear.

When someone passes, we may feel a strong emotional bond with them. We might love or hate them, miss or resent them, miss their physical contact, and often have questions. In my communications with the spirits, they have been intelligent, humorous, compassionate and loving. And they wish to help us live so that when we die, we don't regret our life.

I reread what I wrote, then closed the laptop.

# CHAPTER TEN

FRAMED PHOTOS OF my grandchildren sat in a neat row on my desk. I regretted not seeing Emily, Evan and Lola more often.

Emily was two years old, with curly reddish blonde hair and dark blue eyes like her mother. In the photo she smiled at me with her adorable freckled face. I wished I could see my granddaughter, Nathan and Bridgette more often, but they lived too far away.

Kate's son Evan was turning three next month. He was outgoing, smart and handsome. With his dark hair and dark brown eyes, he resembled his Grandpa Ben. Perhaps my love for Evan can help heal some of my lingering hard feelings toward my ex-husband.

Lola was four years old, smart, lovely and stylish. She liked anything with lace, ribbons or bows and wore decorative clips in her long blonde hair. Would her hair darken or stay as blonde as Kate's, for Lola's once baby blue eyes were now as green as my own.

My grandchildren were beautiful, amazing and full of life. Their futures stretched ahead of them, and I wanted to be a part of their lives. I missed them all, and even though Evan and Lola lived only an hour away, I had not seen them in over a month. This was not the way I wanted it to be. Chad and his grandfather shared a strong bond even after Papaw passed into spirit. I'd like to have that type of bond with my family.

I felt cheated in not having the perfect marriage, and the house with the white picket fence. I longed for a loving husband, caring children and quality time with adoring grandchildren. Instead, I was divorced with no prospects of a partner to share my dreams. My daughter was emotionally detached and my son was geographically distant. And I hated the idea of my grandchildren growing up not knowing me.

I picked up the phone to call Kate, then hung up. Should I call her? What would I say?

Myrtle's message to Carl about calling their son came to mind. Myrtle was right, it wasn't good to not speak with loved ones. I dialed Kate's number, and when she answered I said, "Kate, it's Mom."

"Yes, Mother, I can see that from the caller ID. What's up?"

Why did I need a reason to call? Why couldn't we just chat? My defensive guard was up as I said, "I just called to say hello. How are the children?"

"They're fine."

"That's good, what's new?"

"Nothing much."

Awkward silence. What should I say? "Halloween's almost here, have they picked out their costumes?"

"I'm taking them to the store this afternoon."

"Have they decided what they want to be?"

"Evan wants to be a pirate. And after watching the *Peter Pan* movie the other day, he's decided to dress as Captain Hook."

"Captain Hook, and not Peter Pan?"

"That's right, and it's kind of funny how he pretends to be Hook, but he's calling his sister, *Smee*."

"Smee? Are you referring to Hook's sidekick?"

"Yes, and Lola hates being called that, as you can imagine," she said with a laugh.

"Is Lola dressing as Tinker Bell?"

"No, she's the proverbial princess with her wand, white gloves and tiara. Brad reminded me that she was a princess last year, but I don't see any harm in her being one again."

"No reason I can think of," I said. Silence. "Have you had lunch?"

"Not yet, why?" she said.

"Would you like to meet for lunch?"

"Where would you want to eat?"

"Wherever you want."

Silence. Was she debating going to lunch with me, or where to eat? For being a medium, I sure have a hard time understanding my own family. I guess it's because I'm too emotional about it.

"Okay, and after lunch I'll pick the kids up from daycare to buy their costumes," she said.

I was crestfallen. If they dined with us, I'd get to spend time with them, too, but I knew better than to push. "Okay, if that's easier."

"Yeah, the kids like to eat with their friends. So why don't I..." Kate stopped mid-sentence. The words 'pick you up' hung in the air, suspended between us, left unspoken. I held my breath as I waited for what she'd say next, but she didn't.

"Why don't we meet at the restaurant?" I said.

"Yes, let's do that," she said, sounding relieved. "I'll meet you at The Patio at one o'clock."

Of course she choose The Patio, it had been her favorite restaurant since she was a child. "See you there," I said.

As I hung up the phone, I recalled Red Hawk's message for Jake about the feeling of relief. I didn't want to tote negative emotions to our luncheon, so I asked for spiritual help in ensuring a good visit. I logged off of my computer, closed the desktop and walked out to the storefront.

Megan was gathering her things from the cubby. "Hi, Jennie," she said. "I was just about to remind you that I'm meeting with my counselor today."

"Yes, I remember. So how's it going?"

"You mean here at the store?"

"Yes."

"It's great, and look," she said pointing at a pad of paper on the counter. "I hope you don't mind, but I created a suggestion pad to help encourage and keep track of requests."

"That's a great idea!" I said, impressed by her initiative.

She smiled and said, "And look, someone has written a suggestion."

I read the scrawl, and asked, "What are water labels?"

"Have you heard of Dr. Emoto? He was in the movie *What the Bleep* and he wrote the book, *The Hidden Messages of Water*. He talks about how our emotions affect water."

"Now that you mention it, I do remember him. He published photographs of water crystals reacting to intentions, written and spoken words, and music."

"Yes, that's right. A customer told me about affirmation labels that you stick on your water bottle. When you drink the water, it reflects the vibration of the words on the label, such as peace, joy, love and so on."

"That sounds interesting."

"I thought so too. Can we stock the labels?"

I walked over to Megan's computer and typed a website address in the browser. "This is my sales rep's site. Contact Jim Reslow tomorrow and ask him about the labels, quantities and pricing."

"Okay. So you like my idea?"

"Of the suggestion pad?"

"Yes."

"It's brilliant. Thank you for implementing it."

"I also wanted to tell you that when you decide on your workshop, I can create posters to advertise it." She glanced at her watch. "I gotta go, or I'll be late." She grabbed her books and purse and as she rushed out the door, she said, "I really like it here."

That was good to hear, but I wished Kate liked it here, too.

# CHAPTER ELEVEN

AS I WALKED back to my apartment, I paused at Deanna's office door. Was she giving a reading? Her in-session sign wasn't on the door, so I knocked.

"Come in," Deanna said.

I opened the door and saw her sitting at her desk, frowning and looking troubled. I sat down and asked, "What's wrong?"

"I just had a reading with a Vanessa Bridgestone. When I told her the name of the spirit with us was Rachel, she got angry and said, 'No, not her! I'm not paying you to talk to her!' I thought she would run out of here. In my panic I skipped past the physical description to get to the message."

"Oh, Deanna, it's so important to give the evidential. It's vital that the client acknowledge who we are seeing."

"I know, but Vanessa's reaction flustered me. I asked the spirit for help and viewed a scene where a much younger Vanessa was arguing with Rachel. I couldn't get a sense of how they were related. It felt like Rachel was yet wasn't part of Vanessa's family.

"So I told Vanessa this, and she said Rachel had been her stepmother. She told me her mother had died when she was an infant, and her father married Rachel. She said Rachel was sweet as could be around her father, but cruel to her and her older brother when he wasn't home. I asked Vanessa if Rachel was argumentative and had a quick temper. She said that was an understatement, that Rachel was a horrible person and she's glad she's dead. I felt a tightening in my chest, and asked if Rachel died from a heart attack. Vanessa said she had, which was amazing considering the woman didn't have a heart."

"Did you explain to Vanessa that the spirit of Rachel is no longer that personality?" I said. "Did you tell her how her spirit was coming from a higher energy?"

"No," Deanna said shaking her head. "I didn't get the chance to tell her any of that. And to tell you the truth, I was so unnerved I didn't think of it."

"So what was Rachel's message?" I asked.

"That's when it got really weird."

"How so?"

"When I asked Rachel for the message, she said, 'Tell her I'm dead!' What kind of message is that? Of course she's dead. I hesitated, debating what to do, then told Vanessa that Rachel keeps saying she's dead. As you can imagine, Vanessa looked at me like I was crazy and said, 'Of course she's dead. What a stupid thing to say!'"

"She said that? What happened?"

Deanna flinched at the memory. "I took a calming breath, and received more information. I told Vanessa that Rachel had come because of her concern for her. She said that Vanessa was making herself ill with her own negative emotions."

"How did Vanessa take that?"

"It only made the situation worse. Vanessa screamed at me to tell Rachel to go away! I tried my best to remain calm and connected to spirit, but I felt defensive. Rachel said to tell Vanessa to use her emotions as a tool. But Vanessa's anger frightened me. I feared she'd strike me. Rachel meant to be helpful, but when I repeated her message it made Vanessa angrier. Vanessa stood up so fast she knocked the chair over. She pointed her finger at my face and told me she was not paying to hear from Rachel, or to be told that a ghost was dead. She called me a charlatan, and stormed out of my office. I'll tell you, Jennie, she shook me to my core and I've been sitting here reevaluating my career ever since."

"Oh, Deanna, I'm so sorry you went through that."

"Perhaps it's for the best. I'm in over my head."

"What? You're giving up?"

"Yes, it's an omen."

I was at a loss for words, then remembered something Sara once said. "The medium's job is to give what we get, and you did that, Deanna. It's not up to us that the client likes what they hear."

"Yeah, right," Deanna said, and folded her arms tightly across her chest as she sank deeper into her chair.

'How can I help my friend?' I silently asked my guides, then recalled Deanna's strong Gifts during our training. But she had the tendency to lack confidence. "Deanna, you've given many successful readings. You can't let one session turn you off your path."

Deanna shrugged.

I sensed a spirit in the room. She appeared next to Deanna's chair. "Rachel's here," I said.

Deanna looked startled and said, "Why is she still here?"

"I guess her message wasn't given."

Deanna flushed. "Great, just great," she said. "I did my best, Rachel. I'm sorry if I let you down. I guess I'm just not cut out for this work."

"Oh, Deanna, please stop being so hard on yourself. You are a gifted medium. Rachel is not here to judge you. There's a reason this is happening."

"Yes, there is. It's to show me that I don't belong here," Deanna said, as her eyes filled with tears.

"Maybe you are feeling so emotional right now because of Vanessa."

"What do you mean?"

"Well, you said Rachel was telling Vanessa that she was too emotional. Maybe you absorbed some of it."

Deanna took a deep breath and let out a long sigh. "She certainly overreacted during our session."

"You see? You must be picking up on that energy."

Deanna mulled that over without comment.

It's up to the sitter to choose to take the message, and Vanessa had refused Rachel's. That was her choice. The medium's job is to deliver the message. If Rachel was still here, it meant that Deanna hadn't delivered her entire message.

"We give what we get, Deanna," I said. "Spirit comes in for a reason and we mustn't withhold or judge it."

"But I didn't hold back," Deanna said, her eyes now angry. "I gave what I got."

"Don't take this personally, but there must be more to the message or Rachel wouldn't still be here."

Deanna wiped her tears and blew her nose. "I have some thinking to do."

Regardless, of whether the sitter accepts the message or not, once it is delivered the spirit leaves. If Rachel's still here, it's not because her message wasn't accepted. It's because her message wasn't given. I knew that and so did Deanna.

"Please don't feel so guilty about it, Deanna. You tried your best," I said, then looked at my watch. "I'm sorry, but I have to meet Kate for lunch. Are you going to be okay?"

"Yeah," she said as she sulked.

"Maybe you should call Sara," I said. "She might be able to give you some insight."

She shrugged.

"Well, I do have to run," I said. "Will you be here when I get back?"

"I don't think so. I need some fresh air," she said, and stood up with her tote bag.

We walked out to the front door. Deanna stopped and looked around the store, then at me and said, "I'm sorry, Jennie."

"Sorry for what?"

"You gave me this opportunity, but I'm not ready."

"But you are. You have been doing great. Stop being so hard on yourself. This experience will only make you stronger."

"Yeah, right," she said, and walked out the door.

As I watched Deanna cross the street to her car I became aware of a voice at my ear.

"I'm dead, dead, dead. Tell Vanessa I'm dead," Rachel said.

Oh great, now she was following me!

# CHAPTER TWELVE

RACHEL RODE IN the car with me as I drove to The Patio. "Vanessa didn't get my message," she said.

"Look, Rachel, I'm sorry your message wasn't delivered to Vanessa, but right now I'm going to lunch with my daughter. So please sit tight and I'll catch up with you later, okay?"

Silence. I hoped that meant we had struck a deal. I parked my car and walked up to the restaurant, where the manager greeted me.

"Hello, Ms. Malone. It's wonderful to see you again," Marcus said. He had worked here for as long as I could remember, and had an amazing ability to recall names.

"Hello, Marcus. It's been a while."

"Yes, too long perhaps," he said with a smile.

"Yes, I guess so," I said.

"Miss Kate is waiting for you," he said as he motioned for me to follow him. We walked through the interior of the restaurant as I admired its tropical decor and hand painted walls, chairs and tables. Along the walls and ceiling was a lush array of hanging and potted plants and flowers. We stepped outside to the patio and found Kate already seated at one of the umbrella tables, reading the menu she knew by heart.

Marcus pulled out my chair, and I took a seat. "Thank you, Marcus."

"Would you like a bottle of wine?" he asked.

Kate shook her head.

"No, thank you," I said.

"Enjoy your lunch," he said and summoned our server before walking back into the restaurant.

The waitress came to our table and said, "Hi, I'm Libby. What would you like to drink?"

"Sweet tea," Kate said.

"Ice water with lemon," I said.

Libby walked away, and I looked at my daughter. She had grown into such a beautiful woman. I smiled at her as I unfolded my napkin and placed it in my lap. "Well, this is nice, and I haven't been to The Patio in a while."

"Yes, it is lovely here," she said. "It's still my favorite restaurant."

"It has been your favorite restaurant since you were five years old."

"I guess some things never change," she said.

Libby placed our drinks on the table and opened her order pad. "Have you decided?"

"Yes, I'll have the grilled tuna," Kate said.

"Would you like coleslaw, baked potato or house salad?"

"House salad," Kate said as she handed Libby her menu.

"And for you?"

"I'll have the same," I said.

Libby took our menus and walked away. Kate stirred her drink with a straw and took a sip of the sweet tea.

What should I talk about? It seemed we were always stepping around a mine field when we tried to communicate. "Well, my store's open. It's become a reality," I said as I stepped squarely onto the first explosive.

"I'm thinking of having Evan's birthday party at Live Oak Park," Kate said, abruptly changing the subject.

Why was she disregarding my accomplishment? Her refusals to discuss my life was rude and hurtful. Why can't she be civil and respond? But I didn't confront her.

Instead, I swallowed my anger, knowing I'd pay for it later with indigestion, a sore throat or constipation. "The Park will be nice," I said.

"Yes," she said. "There's the large covered picnic pavilions, the playground and the carousel."

"Does Evan still like to ride the carousel?" I asked. One of my favorite photos is a picture I had taken of him and Lola riding the horses there a few months ago.

"Yes, he and Lola love riding it."

"Well, that sounds like a good plan."

"I just hope the weather is pleasant," she said. "What will I do with ten kids under the age of five if it rains?"

"Bring along some games that they can play in the pavilion."

"That's a good idea," she said and swirled the ice in her glass with the straw.

"Will your father be there?"

Kate nodded. "Of course, and so will Jasmine."

Several years ago Ben married Jasmine. She must be his soul mate for she has brought him emotional stability and has reigned in his bloated ego without breaking his spirit. It was something I had never mastered, and I held a twinge of jealousy about that. But Jasmine had nothing to do with our breakup, we were already divorced when they met. She's been good for Ben, and his art career has soared since she's become his manager.

And not only is she intelligent and cultured, she could have been a model. Jasmine was tall, slender and graceful. She had thick braided black hair, light ebony skin, long thick eyelashes and radiant blue eyes. She was the perfect blend of her Scottish and Jamaican genes.

But what mattered most to me was that Jasmine was kind to my children and grandchildren, and always pleasant to me. So I strived to be civil to her and Ben when we were together, which was at most holidays and family events. So as much as I hated to admit it, I could not find a thing wrong with that woman. And I'd wager that we could have been good friends if she was not married to my ex.

"Earth to Mom," Kate said.

"What?" I asked as she stirred me from my thoughts.

"I said, Are you bringing anyone?"

"Where?"

"Are you bringing anyone to Evan's birthday party?"

"Oh, I don't know. Maybe I'll bring Deanna."

"Deanna?"

"Yes."

"Mom, are you and Deanna...?"

"Deanna and I are just good friends."

"Okay, but if you were more than that, I'd have no problem with it."

Why would she have no problem with that, but was intolerant of my being a medium? "Really? Why would you think that?"

"Well, I haven't known you to date since... well since Richard," she said. "He's the only guy you've dated since you divorced Daddy, isn't he?"

# CHAPTER THIRTEEN

"YOUR FATHER DIVORCED me," I said too quickly and defensively.

Libby brought our lunches. I was grateful to have something to do other than talk about my love life, or lack thereof, with my daughter. I took a long deep breath to quiet my anger before I ate. I needed to learn to not be so defensive, and willed my mind and heart rate to calm.

As I ate, I realize that I had not thought about Richard for some time. Years ago, Richard and his wife, Louisa, had been good friends of ours. Ben and I often went out to dinner with them, or to the movies. We enjoyed hanging out with them and Richard always made us laugh. He had a talent for lightening the mood. And Richard had always been so attentive to Louisa. If she got chilly, he'd get her sweater and place it over her shoulders. Ben was never as thoughtful or caring with me, even when I was pregnant.

A few years after our divorce, I was standing in line at the post office when the person behind me said, "Don't I know you from somewhere?"

I turned around, surprised to see Richard standing there. We gave each other a warm friendly hug, and as the line advanced toward the counter, he asked how I'd been. I told him that Ben and I had divorced, and he said, "Louisa and I have divorced, too."

That surprised me, but I was even more astonished when he said, "Would you like to go out sometime?"

I said, "Yes."

"How about tonight?"

I agreed, then spent the afternoon wondering what to wear. It was silly, what did it matter what I wore? This was just dinner with an old friend, not a date or anything.

That first dinner led to several more. Within the month, we went on a weekend trip to his oceanside timeshare vacation condo. At first, our time together was enjoyable. But within about six months his humor faded to reveal his darker, jaded view of life. He began drinking heavily and ranting about all that was wrong with the world.

My friendly and jovial Richard turned into someone I no longer knew. It's my belief that as energetic beings we magnetize to ourselves at our level of vibration, and I didn't want to align with the dark and dreary future he predicted. I'd try to steer his thoughts and conversation on what's right with the world, but soon I started feeling jaded about life, too. Then one day, in a moment of clarity, I realized that I had to stop living in such a fearful way.

"Richard, we need to talk," I said as I broached the subject. "You are my best friend and I love you, but I can't live like this. We need to rise up in our mindset."

He became defensive and called me sensitive and naive. I told him that we needed time apart. We never did get back together, and I haven't dated anyone since.

I ate my lunch slowly, delaying further conversation with Kate, when she asked, "Well have you?"

"Have I what?"

"Have you been dating?"

"No, Kate, I have not dated anyone since Richard," I said, and selected a roll from the bread basket. And I hadn't wanted to date anyone until I met Jake. An image of him came to mind, and I felt a rush of energy and warmth. For some reason that man had peaked my interest.

"But you broke off with Richard years ago," Kate said. "Don't you miss being in a relationship?"

"I don't have the time."

"But Mom, you're not getting any younger."

"Gee, thanks for pointing that out," I said and tossed the half eaten roll to my empty plate.

Kate bit at her lip, and said, "You need to think... What I mean is, it's not normal to be so alone."

"Why? And who defines normal?"

"You need someone to talk with... and other things," she said, and wiped her mouth with her napkin.

"Other things, Kate? Are you trying to tell me about the birds and the bees?"

Kate laughed. "Someone should; by now you must need a refresher."

"Speaking of relationships, how is Brad?" I asked, turning the conversation off my love life and on to hers.

"He is doing great. He just got a new position at Securata."

"What is Securata?"

"It's one of the world's largest security companies. His cousin, who has worked there for years, added Brad's resume to a job listing there last month. Only he didn't tell Brad. A few days later, Brad got a phone call from a manager at the company asking him to come in for an interview. Fortunately Brad thought quickly and agreed to the appointment. Brad called his cousin who explained that he had submitted his resume, but had forgotten to tell him." Kate took a sip of tea, then said, "Brad went on that interview and got the job!"

"That's great news. Is he happy there?"

"Oh yes, very happy, and it was a great career move. He's been training on their system and next week he'll start updating his sector."

"Wow, he must be smart!"

"Yes, and quite the catch," she said with a laugh.

When Kate met Brad, I liked him right away, and I was thrilled when they married. "Yes, and I like having him in the family, so if you guys ever break up, I'll adopt him."

Kate laughed. "There's no fear of that happening."

They were like two little love birds, kissing and hugging all the time. After eight years of marriage and two children, they were still attentive and affectionate with each other. I wished I could find that in my own life.

Libby brought our check, and I grabbed it.

"What's my share?" Kate asked.

"This is my treat."

"You don't have to do that, Mom."

"I know I don't. Just leave the tip," I said.

"Okay," she said, "but next time it's my treat."

I was glad she had suggested that there would be a next time.

The valet brought her car around. We said goodbye, and I watched Kate drive away. I got into my Subaru and as I turned the key in the ignition, Rachel said, "Tell Vanessa I'm dead."

# CHAPTER FOURTEEN

RACHEL'S PRESENCE GREW stronger as I drove toward Sunflowers, and when I unlocked and opened the front door, she followed me into the store. She was eager to communicate with me as I walked toward my office followed by her familiar chant, "I'm dead, dead, dead. Tell Vanessa."

The only way to get her out of my head, and out of my store, was to get her message delivered. But how had this become my problem? Would Deanna come back and remedy this? It didn't look that way.

From my training I've learned that at some point after death, the spirit sits through a life review. Afterwards, the spirit often seeks to right any wrong, replace error with love and make amends. They desire to inspire, uplift and comfort us with their messages of love and healing.

I sat in my chair, closed my eyes and let my day fall away as I connected with spirit, and asked Rachel to come forward. When I opened my eyes I saw her standing in my office. She had an ivory complexion, red curly hair, and was lovely. She did not look like the raving lunatic I had expected. Instead, she looked quite frustrated in trying to get something done.

She stood before me, hands on hips as she looked squarely into my eyes. Her eyes were not full of rage, but concern. She was not an antagonist, but a concerned spirit desperate to get a message to a loved one.

"I'm ready to help you, Rachel. How may I be of service?"

Rachel's message unfolded as I viewed a scene that reminded me of the one Deanna said she saw. There were two women arguing, Rachel in anger and Vanessa in tears. I sensed this was not the only occurrence. Rachel's need to deliver her message was becoming clearer as I fleshed it out. In finally getting it, I realized its importance. Rachel smiled as I acknowledged her message and why she wanted to get it to Vanessa. But how do I get this message to her stepdaughter? And was it possible to do so while also helping Deanna get her confidence back?

"Rachel," I said, "help me if you can."

Rachel nodded, then faded from view. A different spirit came forward. She was a lovely sprite with vibrant amethyst eyes and what looked like strands of sunbeams in her hair.

"Are you an angel?" I asked.

She smiled and said, "No. I am Mica, your mediumship guide. I have been helping you with your Gifts since you were a child. You knew me then, but you have forgotten. I help you receive and deliver your messages. Think of me as your gatekeeper, coordinating the spirits with your sitters. I have also been helping you connect with spirits in your writing and for the courses that you will teach. I also help you understand your dreams and symbols."

"You help me a lot, thank you," I said. Her presence did feel familiar. "But why have I not seen you till now?"

Mica said, "I've worked in the background until just now when you asked for more help. I am here to assist you."

I was grateful for her and hoped I had not taken her for granted.

As if reading my thoughts, Mica said, "We work as a team and we agreed to do so before your physical birth. Ours is a symbiotic partnership. As you grow spiritually, I grow as well, as do your other guides and spiritual family. Our service is to assist spirits and their sitters."

I felt relieved that I was not alone in my hurdle of delivering Rachel's message.

Mica said, "It is important that Vanessa gets the message so that her healing can begin."

Deanna would be reluctant to contact Vanessa. And how would Vanessa react to such a phone call? How do I get everyone in the same room? How do I approach them? "Can you help me Mica?" I asked, and sensed that I needed to become peaceful. As I meditated, an idea came to mind. It might not be a perfect plan, but it just might work.

I phoned Deanna and asked, "Will you be coming to Sunflowers tomorrow morning?"

"No, I don't belong there."

"But I have something to tell you. Will you come in?"

"What do you have to say?"

"I need to tell you in person."

Deanna sighed. "What time?"

I glanced at my appointment book and said, "How is eleven o'clock?"

"That's fine, I'll be there," she said. "I need to get my things anyway."

As I hung up the phone I said, "Okay Mica. I'll need that help."

# CHAPTER FIFTEEN

THE FOLLOWING MORNING as I opened the front blinds, I looked out at the torrential downpour. It never ceased to amaze me how quickly after a hard rain, there's barely a puddle due to the water flowing into the aquifer beneath the state.

But there were puddles now as a red Toyota Corolla pulled into the parking lot. The door opened and Megan dashed out, and ran across the flooded street. I opened the front door for her and she stepped onto the entry mat and shook off her rain-soaked parka.

"Think we'll get rain?" I said.

Megan laughed. "Oh yeah, I think we might get some." She walked behind the front counter and stowed her things, then turned on the cash register and the lighting in the display case.

After she settled in at her desk, I said, "Megan, I need a favor."

"Sure, what is it?"

"Please call this woman and ask her to come in to see me at eleven-thirty. Tell her it's an urgent matter," I said as I handed her a piece of paper.

"Okay."

"And please don't make any other appointments until later today or tomorrow. Oh, and I have someone coming in at nine."

"Okay," Megan said as she picked up the phone to place the call.

My first appointment would arrive soon. After that, my focus will be on my eleven o'clock meeting.

☼

Evelyn promptly arrived at nine and sat across from me at my reading table. She had shoulder length brown hair and wore a gray skirt, a white lace trimmed blouse, a gray sweater and black high heels. She dressed professionally; perhaps she was a banker, a realtor or an attorney.

She dabbed at her eyes which were swollen and red from crying. The saturated tissue fell in small pieces to her lap. I pushed the tissue box closer to her, and she pulled out several sheets.

I had been waiting for her to collect herself, but from the way she was sobbing, I doubted she ever would.

"Would you like some water?"

She nodded yes.

I brought her a bottled water, and sat down again as I said, "Let's begin."

Evelyn nodded.

I connected with the spirit realms and a woman's spirit appeared behind Evelyn's chair. She looked somewhat like Evelyn, but older. "Is your mother in spirit?"

Evelyn nodded and wiped at her tears. "Yes," she said.

I described her and said, "She was full of humor and genuinely liked people. She was on the stage when she was young, and loved to sing and dance. She was quite an entertainer."

"Yes, that's true," Evelyn said, and took a calming breath.

"She gave up the stage when she married."

"Yes."

"She raised only you, she had no other children."

"That's right," she said.

I felt heaviness in my chest, and I struggled for breath. "She had problems with her lungs. Did she pass from emphysema?"

"Yes," she said.

The symptoms passed with her acknowledgment, and I took a grateful breath. "She brings forth another child. But this wasn't hers?" Something felt off, and I said, "Did you lose a child?"

Evelyn burst into tears and wailed so loudly, her body shook with emotions.

*'What just happened?'* I silently asked my guide.

"Give her a moment to calm down," Mica said.

The spirits of the mother and the child hugged Evelyn, who was oblivious to their presence.

Mica said, "This was Evelyn's pregnancy."

"Why have you feared your mother being with this baby?"

"She never knew I was having sex with my boyfriend and I never told her I got pregnant," Evelyn said. "My boyfriend and I were deciding what to do about it, when I miscarried. I was glad she'd never find out, but when she died I realized she would."

Evelyn's mother and child smiled at me. "Your mother is with the baby," I said, "who is coming to me not as an infant, but as a toddler. Your mother is with him, tending to him. They both love you. There is no reason to fear your mother."

"But my mother must be furious!" Evelyn said.

The mother's spirit smiled as she held the hand of the grandchild she hadn't known in the flesh. "No, Evelyn," I said, "she is not angry. During her lifetime, she might have reacted that way, but in spirit she does not. She is with him and they both watch over you and send you love."

Evelyn's face transformed from pinched with fear to relaxed and peaceful. It was as if a new person sat in her chair, her fears lifted.

Evelyn said, "They are together?"

"Yes."

"Will I ever see them again?"

"Yes, they will greet you on the other side when your time comes."

Evelyn breathed a sigh of relief as her mother and child faded from the room.

"You can't change the past," I said. "But you do create your future, so don't create with fear. Do you know what fear is?"

Evelyn shrugged.

"Fear is false-evidence-appearing-real. You have been living with the fear of your mother finding out about the child. Know that she is with him and they both love you, so you can release that fear now."

"Thank you," she said.

When the session ended, Evelyn hugged me. She looked happy, lighter and younger than when she first walked into my office. The ways in which spirit works never ceases to amaze me.

☼

After Evelyn left, I asked, '*Is Kate keeping anything from me?*'

Mica said, "Don't go there."

My guide was right. I had sworn to not use mediumship to intrude on my family's personal issues unless they specifically asked for my help.

Megan stepped into the doorway. "I made that phone call. She said she'd be here by eleven-fifteen. She wanted more information, but I told her I had none to give." She looked puzzled.

"I purposely didn't give you any details. I'll explain later. Please let me know when she arrives."

# CHAPTER SIXTEEN

THE FRONT DOOR wind chimes pealed out, and I looked at the time. Ten forty-five, must be Deanna. I felt a shiver of anticipation. Here goes nothing. Deanna was speaking with Megan, but I couldn't hear what they were saying from my office. A few moments later, Deanna stood at my doorway.

"Good morning," I said.

"Morning," she said, "now what's this about?"

"Close the door and have a seat."

She sat down, looking tired.

"How are you?" I asked.

"I'm still shaken by what happened, so I've decided to take another offer."

"Oh? What is it?"

"It's with an organization that works on cold cases. I won't meet with clients. They'll send me paperwork on missing persons and unsolved cases and all I have to do is write down my impressions."

"Sounds interesting, but I do wish you wouldn't quit your practice here just because of one session."

"It's an omen. I wasn't sure if I was ready for this, and I'm not. I still shudder at how Rachel screamed she was dead and Vanessa yelled at me. It's like a loop playing in my mind and I can't get past it."

"Let's see if I can help," I said, knowing that in her agitated state it would be difficult for spirit to connect with her. She took a deep breath and closed her eyes as I led her in a guided meditation. When she opened her eyes, she appeared more relaxed. "Okay, now I have something to tell you. After you left here yesterday, Rachel started following me."

"You're kidding!" Deanna said, shifting uncomfortably in her chair.

"No cause for alarm," I said. "Let me finish. I was meeting Kate, so I asked Rachel to be patient, and she was. But after lunch, Rachel was waiting, and I sat for the message she wants to give her stepdaughter."

"I told Rachel I was sorry," Deanna said, her eyes misting.

"Don't get upset, let's not go in that direction. Okay? Cause there's more I have to tell you."

"Oh?"

"Yes, I had Megan phone Vanessa and ask her to come here this morning. She said she'd be here at eleven-fifteen."

Deanna sat up alarmed. "What? She's coming here?"

"Yes, and so is Rachel."

"You tricked me, Jennie! Why are you doing this to me?"

"Because I believe that Rachel's message is important. And our work as mediums is not about us; it's about serving spirit. So even if you don't want to work here, and that's your choice, I hope that in seeing this through you'll realize the value of your Gifts."

Deanna shrugged. "Okay. Is Rachel here now?"

"You tell me," I said and watched Deanna close her eyes, to connect so that she could communicate with Rachel.

Deanna nodded her head as if listening to someone. She opened her eyes and said, "You are right. This is important. But will Vanessa listen?"

I was grateful to see the shift in Deanna's attitude, from self-pity and fear, back to being of service. "That's not up to us, but I hope she does."

The front door chimes rang out again and my stomach flipped; the moment of truth. I heard Megan stop outside my door, hesitating.

"Did you hang up your in-session sign?" Deanna said.

"Oh, I forgot," I said and went to the door and opened it.

"Your next appointment's here," Megan said with a nod toward the storefront. "And I have to leave for school by noon. You want me to lock up when I leave?"

"Yes, Megan, thank you. Please bring in Vanessa."

Deanna looked at me and smiled. We may have both felt a bit nervous, but knew that this was up to spirit. We just hoped to get past her defenses to get through this.

The door to my office opened as Megan said, "Jennie's in here."

Vanessa walked into the room, and looked surprised to see Deanna seated there. "What's this about?" she asked.

"Welcome, Vanessa. Please have a seat," I said pointing to the chair next to Deanna.

Vanessa sat stiffly on the edge of the chair, her purse propped on her lap. She looked as if she was about to bolt from the room. Not sure how to begin, I said, "I understand you left here upset yesterday."

Vanessa glared at Deanna and said, "That's an understatement."

"Yes, well it was quite unfortunate," I said, "but if you'll hear me out, I have something to tell you."

# CHAPTER SEVENTEEN

VANESSA TURNED TOWARD me and said, "What do you want to tell me?"

I silently asked Rachel to help me to accurately deliver her message, and in a way Vanessa would hear it. But as I was about to speak, Deanna spoke instead, so I remained silent.

"Rachel..." As soon as Deanna mentioned the name, Vanessa glared at her, her body tensed and her face flushed.

"Not this again! I won't stand for it," Vanessa said and stood from the chair.

"Please, hear us out," I said.

Vanessa paced, then perched on the seat's edge. I decided to pick up the pace so we could deliver the message before she fled the room.

"Rachel told us we had to give you her message or she won't leave," I said.

"What? What do you mean?"

"After you and Deanna left yesterday, Rachel gave me her message."

"She did?"

"Yes, she has been here since yesterday."

Vanessa looked around the room with alarm. "She's here now?"

"Yes, she is with us now and she wants us to tell you something."

Vanessa sat quietly, looking unsure of how to react.

Deanna leaned toward her as she said, "Please, Vanessa, listen. Let me get this out. She really wants you to get this message, and I'm asking her to help me deliver it to you accurately." Deanna paused for a breath, then continued. "I told you I felt a tightening in my chest, which you confirmed to be her death from a heart attack."

"Yes, that's right."

"So she's dead," Deanna said quickly.

"What is this, some kind of joke?" Vanessa asked.

"No, please let me finish. What I kept hearing from Rachel, but was reluctant to say was, 'I am dead, dead, dead.' Rachel wants you to really get that she is dead. She is no longer in the flesh."

Vanessa was quiet a moment, then said, "So I'm to just forget everything? She's dead so I just forgive her?"

I now realized why there was such urgency to Rachel's message. Deanna seemed to be at a loss as to what to say.

I said, "The person you knew as Rachel, the woman you are angry with, is no longer alive. She shed that personality at death, and it no longer exists! She's gone home to spirit and has healed on a soul level."

"Well, good for her," Vanessa said, and sat back in her chair, arms crossed.

"But she wants you to heal, too," I said. As I delivered more of the message chills ran up and down my arms. Rachel was happy that the message was accurate.

Vanessa grew quiet. I looked at her and hoped she would not scream at us or get upset. "Okay, so she's never coming back here. She's dead. I don't have to fear her anymore. I don't have to deal with Rachel anymore. Is that what you are saying?"

"Yes," I said. "The personality and the person you knew as Rachel is gone. She is dead. Your relationship with her is over. You can let it go. You no longer need be emotionally bound to or upset by it. You are free to create a new future."

Vanessa's features softened as she uncrossed her arms, and let out a sigh. She looked from me to Deanna and said, "Thank you. I get it. That was a good message."

I felt so relieved I almost collapsed. Rachel smiled and faded from view, her message delivered.

Vanessa stood from her chair and said, "Thank you for calling me back here. I almost didn't come, but something urged me to do so. All the way here I was unsure I'd enter your store again, but it was as if an invisible hand was pushing me. I'm glad I came. Thank you both."

I smiled. That invisible hand likely belonged to Mica. I followed Vanessa out to the storefront. She surprised me by taking several of my business cards. I unlocked the front door, and she said, "I'll tell my friends. Thanks again."

I returned to my office to find Deanna smiling.

She hugged me and said, "I'm still unsure it's right for me to be here. I think I will work for a while with the cold case files, and maybe someday I'll try this again."

"You are welcome here whenever you want."

Deanna walked into her office and packed her things. I walked with her to the front door. She hugged me again, not saying a word, then left.

As I watched her walk to her car, I was saddened she would no longer be working here with me. But happy she would continue using her Gifts. In facing Vanessa and delivering Rachel's message, Deanna had overcome her ordeal.

I locked the door and stood with my back to it. It's when we get out of the way, and let go of fears, that we become a conduit for the messages.

Rachel's message applied to my life, too. My father and I had a challenging relationship. I had always sought his approval, which was never forthcoming. I wasted years being insecure and afraid to live my dreams, even after he passed away. Always fearful of what he'd think, always afraid of his reproach. Rachel's message had not only been healing for Vanessa, but for me, too. It was true what Sara had said, "The message heals both the sitter and the medium." The spirit of Rachel had left my store, but her message had healed my heart.

I had two more appointments that afternoon. The spiritual lift that I felt from Rachel's message raised me to new heights, energizing those readings.

# CHAPTER EIGHTEEN

I WAS LOCKING the storefront after my last appointment when there was a knock on the door. I peeked out the window. What's he doing here? I unlocked the door and said, "Hi, Jake, what's up?"

"Have you had dinner yet?"

"No, I was going to make a sandwich," I said.

"Well, would you like to go get something to eat?"

As I gazed into his vibrant blue eyes, I experienced that same strong attraction I felt during his reading. Did he feel it too? "Where did you have in mind?"

"Ever eat at The Patio?"

I laughed. "I ate there yesterday."

He looked surprised.

"I had lunch with my daughter," I said, wanting to make that clear.

"Well, how about the Crab Shack?"

I liked that rustic and charming riverfront restaurant, and jumped at the chance to be near water. "Sounds great, let me grab my purse." He stood at the door as I started walking toward my apartment. I stopped and turned around. "Come on in," I said, "I'll just be a minute."

Jake stood in the waiting area while I rushed back to my apartment. I quickly freshened up, checked my appearance in the mirror and grabbed my purse. I nearly skipped down the hallway, feeling as lighthearted and giddy as a schoolgirl.

Jake opened the front door for me, and waited as I locked it. We walked to his black Jeep Wrangler, and he opened the passenger door. I slid onto the leather seat and he closed my door. I watched him walk around to the driver's side and sit down. He had certainly impressed me by his thoughtful manners. Jake smiled at me, and I relaxed.

He backed out of the parking lot and as we headed east toward the river I tried to think of something to talk about. He must have wondered the same thing for he turned on the radio and asked, "You like music?"

"Yes, I like most music."

"You like country music?"

"Some of it," I said. "I like Sugarland, Rascal Flatts, Keith Urban and Kenny Chesney."

"Doesn't everyone like Chesney?" he said with another smile. "Do you like rock?"

"I like soft classic rock and some jazz."

"Ever go to the Hard Rock for a concert?"

"No, where is that?"

"It's at Downtown Disney," he said. "We'll go sometime."

I thrilled at the idea of his making future plans for us, when a small voice piped in to remind me that we hadn't even shared a meal yet. But as the miles passed by, the more relaxed I became, and told that small fearful voice to take a hike. I rather liked sitting next to Jake Walker. It felt natural to be with him, like I'd known him my whole life. Or was it lifetimes? Perhaps.

Jake parked at the restaurant and escorted me inside. I've eaten there a dozen times or more, but with Jake it was a new experience. We sat at a table with a view of the river. The waitress handed us menus and asked what we would like to drink.

"I'll have a glass of Riesling," I said.

Jake said, "Make that a bottle and bring two glasses."

We looked over our menus. There were few choices, but each selection was freshly caught and delicious. The waitress returned with the glasses and brought the bottle of wine in a bucket of ice. She poured a small amount of wine into Jake's glass. He expertly swirled the wine, took a sip and nodded his approval. She poured wine into both of our glasses and asked if we were ready to order. I ordered the seafood platter and Jake ordered the snapper. The waitress took our menus and said, "I'll be right back with your salads and fresh rolls."

Jake raised his wine glass to mine, and we clinked glasses as he said, "It's nice being with you."

"You too, and thank you for asking me to dinner."

"My pleasure," he said. We sipped our drinks as we gazed out at the river. A sailboat anchored near the bridge waited for it to open, while several pontoons and other boats motored by. Jake said, "Have you heard that the St. John's and the Nile are the only two rivers that run north?"

"Yes, I have heard that."

"I've read that its just a common belief and that most rivers run north. The article I read said that the St. John's River runs north and south depending on gravity, topography and geology. The river simply follows the path of least resistance along its 300 mile journey."

"I did not know that; that's interesting."

"Did you ever ride on the river?"

"No, I always wanted to have a boat, but Ben wasn't interested. I wouldn't want to ride on my own now."

"We'll have to rent a boat and take a long ride. Would you like that?"

"Yes, I would," I said, thrilled again that he saw a future with us together.

"One of the things on my bucket list is to travel the Okeechobee Waterway. You launch the boat in near Stuart, cross Lake Okeechobee about midway, then continue west to Fort Myers. The ride across the State would take two or more days, depending on the locks and bridges and how fast you rode."

Was he inviting me to join him? It could be fun.

There was a group of people pole fishing on the far bank near an anchored pontoon boat. One of the men pulled a fish from the water. Jake broke the silence as he said, "I'd like to get to know you better, Jen. Is it okay to call you Jen?"

"Yes, that's fine," I said, enjoying how my name sounded when he spoke it. "What would you like to know about me?"

"Everything," he said with a smile, then added, "Someone told me you're not married."

"Oh? You asked about me?"

"Yes, look, Jen, I'm not a school boy and I don't play games. Well, other than golf that is," he said with a laugh, then knitted his brow. "I like to be upfront."

"I don't like to play games either," I said.

"Well, when you said that you golfed years ago with your husband, I assumed..."

"You assumed I was still married. And I didn't say anything to clear that up, did I?"

"No, you didn't."

I took a sip of wine as I debated how to respond. "You were there for an appointment. I didn't think it was good business to flirt with my client."

He laughed. "Maybe a little flirting would be good for business."

I laughed. "Could be," I said, then shook my head, "But no, not really." I sat quiet a moment, then said, "Well, it's true, I'm not married. We divorced several years ago."

"Any children?"

"Yes, I have a daughter and a son. Kate is married to Brad, and Nathan is married to Bridgette. And I've been blessed with three grandchildren, Emily, Evan and Lola. How about you?"

"No. We tried, but couldn't."

"Oh, I'm sorry to hear that," I said.

He shrugged. "Well, who knows? We were happy enough, just the two of us. We had a number of good years until Connie... until the cancer."

"I'm sorry for your loss." I patted his forearm and a spark bit my hand. The man was so electrifying.

"Thanks, and thanks for letting me know that Connie's okay."

I pulled my hand from Jake's arm. "You are welcome. Glad to be of service," I said, and wondered if Connie was here with us now.

"It was a relief to get a message from her," he said.

"That's why I do what I do."

"Well, it's a good thing to be doing," Jake said, and sipped his wine, "but how do you do it?"

"I'm sort of like a transceiver. I see, hear or sense the spirits, and narrate what they tell or show me."

"That's quite amazing."

"Yes, I guess it is. I don't take it for granted, but rather I'm in constant awe of how intelligent and loving and on target the messages from spirit are. It's quite amazing to bear witness to."

"Are you sensing any spirits with us now?"

"No, I'm not connected. I mean, I have intuition like everyone else, but I don't stay tapped into the spirit realms all day."

"I guess that would wear you out."

"While I enjoy the connection, I tend to lose a sense of space and time. Staying connected too long can make me spacey. I need down time as I have to live in this world, too."

# CHAPTER NINETEEN

JAKE FILLED OUR glasses and said, "I can understand that. I guess that's true in most professions, except golf."

I laughed. "I imagine even pro golfers need their rest."

"Yes, that's true," he said.

It was dark out, and the moonlight reflected on the surface of the river. Not as many boats were traveling now. The river had taken on a different ambience after the sun set.

"So do your kids live nearby?" he asked.

"Nathan lives in Ohio, so I don't get to see them much."

"That is quite a drive from here."

"Yes, and my daughter and her family live an hour away."

"That's closer, you see them much?"

"Not as often as I'd like."

"Why's that?"

I blushed. "My daughter doesn't approve of my career."

He looked surprised. "Why not?"

"I'm not entirely sure, but she's made it clear that she won't come to the store. And she won't talk about it."

"That's a shame. She must not understand the value of what you do. You helped me and I've heard of how you've helped others."

That was a surprise. "You've heard talk about me?"

"Yes, word gets around," he said with a smile. "Relax. It's all good."

I pondered that as our food arrived.

As we ate he said, "As I mentioned, I'd like for us to get to know each other."

"I'd like that, too, so tell me about yourself, Jake."

"Well, I was raised in Alpharetta, Georgia."

"You're from Georgia? I don't detect an accent."

"I guess I lost it sometime after high school. I went to college in California. After graduation I enlisted in the Navy. When my enlistment was up, I traveled around the states and Canada for about a year. When I returned to Georgia I married Connie. I haven't dated much since Connie passed. We were friends since childhood so when she died I lost not only my wife, but my best friend. Her bout with cancer had been difficult and watching her die nearly killed me. After she passed away, I spent time alone up at the cabin. That helped me get through it."

"The cabin? Where is that?"

"In the north Georgia mountains."

"There's mountains in Georgia? Isn't Georgia just flat fields, red clay, peanuts, and Atlanta?"

"There's all that and much more. There's mountains, lakes, rivers and waterfalls. It's beautiful country and not just cotton fields and peanut farms."

"I had no idea. So was the cabin you stayed at yours?"

"It is now. My parent's left me their cabin on the lake."

"It sounds lovely. Why didn't you stay there?"

"Well, after Connie first passed away, I wanted to be alone. I didn't want to talk to anyone or pretend I was okay. I enjoyed being by myself and spending time alone outdoors and in nature. I'd fish or hike or just look at the water. The area is beautiful in any season, but after a while it got too quiet and I stopped enjoying my solitude. So I came back to Florida. Connie and I had a home here several years ago, and we liked it. And the weather allows me to golf all year. And I haven't dated much. I guess you could say I'm quite particular about who I spend my time with."

I was surprised by his remark, was that a compliment?

After we finished our meals and the waitress cleared the plates, Jake held my hand and said, "I'd like to see you again."

"I'd like that, too," I said, enjoying the feel of my hand in his. "Do you like birthday parties?"

"That depends. Whose birthday?"

"It's Evan's birthday next week. He'll be three. Would you like to come?"

"To your grandson's birthday party?" he said pulling his hand away.

"Why not? It'll be fun."

"Yeah?"

"Yes, and you'll meet my daughter and son-in-law and my ex and his wife."

"That should be interesting. Will anyone else be there?"

"Yes, me," I said.

His eyes softened. "Count me in."

Jake drove us back to Sunflowers. I liked being with him and was sorry for the evening to end. But I was grateful we had dined together. It had been a lovely evening.

Jake parked in front of my store and turned off the ignition. We unhooked our seat belts and turned toward each other. "I hope you had a good time."

"I did, thank you for asking me."

He smiled as he took my hand. "So what gift should I get Evan?"

"You don't have to bring him a gift. You're coming as my guest," I said holding his hand and enjoying him being so near.

"I think there's a rule about no cake or ice cream without a gift. Does Evan like golf?"

"He's going to be three. I doubt he's aware of golf."

"It's never too young to start."

"Whatever you want to bring is fine."

Jake smiled as he leaned toward me. He smelled wonderful. I leaned closer and as our lips met, we lingered. His kiss was warm and tender. I pulled back and held his gaze, my energy blending with his. Jake had to be a kindred soul. How else was it possible to love a man I just met? He leaned in and we held the kiss longer this time. We sat back smiling at each other.

I reluctantly stepped from the Jeep, and he escorted me to the sidewalk. He waited while I unlocked the door. I stepped in the doorway and turned toward him. "Thank you again. I had a good time." He took my hand. Another minute and he'll be in my bed. But this was proceeding too quickly. I had to catch my breath.

Jake seemed to be debating his next move. "I had a good time, too. I like being with you and getting to know you."

"Me, too," I said and placed my palm on his chest, "but I need to take this slowly."

His face was alive with a passion he held in check. "I don't want to push you. I'm willing to give this more time if that's what you need."

"Yes, I just need some time."

"I understand," he said, then leaned in with another kiss.

Passion swelled in me and I ached for him. If I don't stop now I'll be dragging him to my bed. I pulled back and said, "Good night, Jake."

He smiled and nodded. "Good night. See you Sunday."

"Sunday?"

"For the party?"

"Oh, yes, Evan's birthday. That'll be great."

"What time should I pick you up?"

"Noon."

"See you then."

Jake walked to his Jeep as I closed and locked the front door, and leaned against it. I burned with desire for him and it took all my will power to not open the door and call him to me. The man was electrifying!

# CHAPTER TWENTY

I HAD SUCH a strong attraction toward Jake, but was I ready for a relationship? Did he play a role in this new phase of my life? Did I have the time to give to him, when I'm so busy building my new business?

I sat at my desk thinking about our date. Jake had been the perfect gentleman the entire evening. He's a good listener, and easy to be with. And his kiss! We would've spent a passionate night of lovemaking if I'd said yes.

I doodled his name on a piece of paper, then flinched with panic and dropped the pen. Had I really invited him to Evan's birthday party? What was I thinking? Did I want him to meet the family after only one date? Had I put him on the spot? Why had he agreed to go?

It's much easier giving messages to my clients. I simply connect with spirit in a detached sort of way, without judgment or expectation. But when it comes to my life's questions, I'm prone to judge any guidance I receive. It's much harder to be emotionally detached for myself.

But I needed answers. '*Was Jake in my future?*' I asked as I settled back in my chair and closed my eyes, willing myself to suspend judgment. I took several deep breaths, asked for guidance and plugged into spirit.

When I opened my eyes, I expected to see a spirit with me. Instead I saw a vision of a large book falling from the sky and landing on my desk. It looked to be an ancient tome.

"This is the *Akashic Record*," Mica said. "This has all your life experiences, both past and future events. We are scanning the pages for your answer."

The heavy ornate cover opened, and the pages flipped as if someone was searching for something. The pages stopped turning, and I looked at the illustrated scene from the 1600s. A man and a woman stood side by side in front of a log cabin. The woman wore a long-sleeved floor length dress and a white apron. She wore a white bonnet on her head and cradled an infant in her arms. The man was clad in dark trousers, a long sleeved shirt and a brown suede vest. He held a rifle at his side, its stock resting on the ground.

"Who were they?" I asked and the image zoomed nearer. Even though it did not look like us now, this was Jake with me in a past life.

The image zoomed out, and the pages flipped again and stopped. The page held an image of me in this lifetime. Standing next to me was a man, his features nondescript. "Is that Ben?" I asked.

"No," Mica said.

"Is it Jake?"

"Could be," Mica said.

"You're not going to tell me?"

"The future is for you to create. We are showing you that you did allow for a relationship at this stage of your life. We are showing you a possibility, but what happens will reflect the choices you make."

"So it's okay for me to pursue a relationship with Jake?"

"There is no right or wrong. It is up to you and Jake to create your realities."

"So should I go ahead and date him?"

"You know better than to ask a 'should' question. There are no shoulds. We are showing you what is possible. And we have shown you that you were together in a past life. But you have free will."

Like many of my clients, I often wished our guides told us what to do. But then they wouldn't be our guides, they'd be our masters and overlords. So as much as I wanted Mica to foretell my future, it's my fate to decide.

"Okay, Mica. I got your message," I said.

The voluminous book closed and returned to the shelves of the Akashic Library.

I pondered Jake. It felt natural, grounded, comfortable and safe to be with him. And when I was not with him, I longed to be with him again. So if I used my emotions like a tool, as Red Hawk had said, being with Jake felt better. And I liked that Jake allowed me to be myself. He even said he didn't like to play games. He wasn't like Richard or Ben. Instead of chaos, Jake offered a calm harbor. It felt safe to drop anchor and let my boat bobble next to his, protected from emotional riptides and tsunamis.

I needn't wear a false face, and he seemed comfortable in his own skin. We could allow each other to be authentic, which was empowering and brought a sense of relief; and felt powerfully sexy.

I didn't know if Jake would stay anchored a long time in my harbor, but for now, I liked the idea of mooring next to him.

# CHAPTER TWENTY-ONE

THE NEXT MORNING I sat at my desk, recollecting every moment of last night's date. I touched my fingers to my lips as I recalled our lingering kisses, and sighed. Jake seemed too good to be true. I was smitten and smiling a lot this morning. The man was having an effect on me.

But I needed to get down to business, and I logged onto my laptop and opened a new document. I had decided to write about my mediumship experiences, I just wasn't yet sure whether to fictionalize it. So I sat with my hands perched at the keyboard, in indecision. I'll just get it all down, then figure out how to proceed. As I typed I lost track of time, and got lost in my tale. So it took a minute to realize that Megan was standing at my door. I turned to look at her.

"New client," she said with a nod toward the storefront.

"Okay, thanks," I said, and closed my desk. I followed her down the hall to the front counter. A woman, perhaps in her late fifties, was standing there. She must have been a young beauty, because she was still striking for her age. She was ultra-thin in her belted skinny jeans and tucked in shirt. She wore her waist length brown hair gathered in a long ponytail, and it was a good look on her.

She smiled at me as I approached, and said, "Are you Jennie Malone?"

"Yes, I am," I said.

"My Uncle Carl told me about seeing you," she said. Her uncle had been my first, if unofficial, client. "How is he doing?" I asked.

"Actually, that's why I'm here," she said.

"Oh? Come with me and we'll talk in my office."

She followed me down the hallway, and took a seat at the table. I closed the door, grabbed a pen and paper and sat opposite her. "You were saying you are here because of Carl. Is something wrong?"

"No, he's doing fine. Real fine," she said, nodding her head. "I hadn't seen my uncle for months, so imagine my surprise when I visited him the other day. There was such a change in his manner that I finally came right out and asked him about it. He told me about his visit with you and his message from Aunt Myrtle. I was about to debunk it," she said with a shrug, "but then thought, whatever happened had changed him for the better. In fact, I can't get over the improvement. He's gone from a cranky old grouch to a happy old man who is always smiling. I wanted to stop in and thank you for that."

"Well, thank you for letting me know, um," I stammered. She hadn't given me her name.

She blushed, "Oh, please forgive my manners. My name is Joyce Dillon, but all my friends call me JD."

"It's nice to meet you, JD. Thank you for telling me how well your uncle is doing, but I give all the credit to the spirits. I'm just an instrument, a channel for helping them get their messages delivered."

"Well, I don't know about any of that. But I'm impressed by the improvement in my uncle's manner and disposition," she said, then leaned toward me. "So I hoped you could help me, too."

"How can I help you?"

"I've been forgetting things. When I tell my friends about it, they laugh and say they're getting forgetful too. But they're talking about lost keys and forgotten appointments. You know," she said with a shrug, "things like that. I don't discuss it further with them because I don't want them to know how bad it's getting. I'm ashamed, I guess."

"Ashamed of what?"

She looked down at her hands as she nervously rubbed them together. I noticed she had bitten her nails to the quick. "When I forget keys and stuff like that, I can laugh it off. But the other day I forgot my daughter-in-law's name. I mean, Meredith's been a part of our family for over 20 years. She's as close to me as my own daughter, and I forgot her name!"

"Oh, how awful for you," I said.

"That's not the worst of it," she said as she grabbed a tissue from the box on the table. Her skin reddened as she wiped away her tears. "Yesterday was the worst day of my life! I forgot my grandchild's name. Oh, I'm so ashamed. What kind of grandmother would do that?"

What a terrible thing to experience! I could understand why she was so upset. It would be dreadful to forget any of my grandchildren's names.

"Can you help me?" she asked. "Seeing the change in Uncle Carl, I hoped you could give me some insight."

"Well, I can't do anything for you as I don't have your answers. But we can see what guidance or advice the spirits offer. You know, this could be stress, but I encourage you to see your doctor. Okay?"

She nodded and said, "Okay."

I connected to spirit, and immediately sensed an older woman standing behind JD's chair. I told JD, and said, "She looks somewhat like you, but she has short gray hair, and she is not as tall as you. She stands in my symbolic place for grandmother. No wait," I said as the spirit took two steps up. "She was your great grandmother. She is showing me a scene where she is baking pies. The view from her kitchen window is of her yard and several fruit trees. I'm getting the sense that her home was by the Great Lakes," I said as the spirit showed me a map. "She was either in Michigan or Ohio."

"That's right, her side of the family was from Traverse City," JD said.

The scene changed, and there was a haze of smoke around the grandmother. The smoke grew denser, and I was choking. Barely able to speak or take a breath, I said, "Did she die in a fire?"

"So I was told. Her older brother had been visiting, and he fell asleep while smoking and caught her house on fire. Daddy said she died in her sleep." JD placed her hand to her chest as she leaned toward me and said, "Did she suffer?"

My choking stopped, and I took a grateful deep breath. "No, her spirit released while she slept, she didn't suffer at all."

The grandmother showed me a new scene of a little girl. *'Was this a young JD?'* I asked.

The spirit nodded, indicating that it was. In the scene, JD looked upset as she watched her parents drinking and arguing. I sensed this was a common, perhaps daily routine. Their arguing escalated, and her father hit her mother on the head with a whiskey bottle. The woman fell unconscious to the floor.

# CHAPTER TWENTY-TWO

I HESITATED TO repeat this to JD. But trained to give what I get I said, "I see a scene before me where people are fighting. It's your parents."

"Oh, yes," she said with a wave of her hand, "I guess they fought all the time."

"But in this scene, he struck her on the head with a bottle."

Tears spilled from her eyes. "My grandparents told me I was there when he killed her. I was a toddler, and I don't remember them or the incident. Guess I've blocked it all from my memory. He went to prison for it and died while in there."

"I'm so sorry," I said, then saw that JD had lived a hard life. She had a history of abusive men and addiction to drugs and alcohol. But she wasn't in a relationship now, and she was sober and cleaning up her act. As I sat watching, listening and sensing all that her grandmother gave me, the clairomniscience kicked in. I got and understood the message. Her grandmother nodded at me, indicating that I had indeed received it.

"Your grandmother says she is helping guide you, and celebrates your efforts to change your life for the better. She suggests nutritional counseling to help repair your body. And she tells me that you have become proficient at forgetting your past."

JD nodded, "I guess that's true."

"She says that forgetting your past is... how do I say this? It's a survival mechanism, and is contributing to your current state of forgetfulness. Your grandmother is showing me a blackboard. She writes on it with chalk, then wipes it clean. She is illustrating your erasing the slate of your mind's memories."

JD sat to attention. "You mean I'm doing that with my own family? Oh, how awful! I love them; I don't want to do that!"

"I don't think it's intentional. You're not consciously forgetting your daughter-in-law or anyone else that you love. It's more a habit that's the cause of what's going on."

JD dabbed at her eyes. "Really?"

"You've created this habit, by giving your mind a command. It's like installing software in a computer. It's automatically clearing your memory banks. It's a coping mechanism for forgetting past events and you've been doing this most of your life."

"But why?"

"Because it gives you a sense of relief, which reinforces the mechanism. You had good reasons when you created this pattern, but you never shut the program down. It's still running in the background. The software is doing what you programmed it to do long ago. But it's not selective. It erases everything on autopilot."

JD looked alarmed. "How do I stop it?"

"Good question," I said, and asked her grandmother. "Your grandmother says you need to see a therapist who can help you recover from your past so you can shut down the program. Tell the therapist what we discussed. I'm getting that hypnotherapy could be useful. When you feel safe enough to stop the habit, you will do so."

"How will I find this therapist?"

"Spirit is guiding you. Be open to synchronicity. You might hear a name on the radio or in conversation; or see a photo in the news or online. If you are paying attention, you will get a sense of who is the right person; one who is open to this idea and able to help you. Just trust the process. Something about the person will catch your attention."

JD's grandmother kissed the top of her head, smiled at me and faded from view. "Your grandmother has kissed you goodbye, her message has been delivered."

"This was helpful, and what you said about the program makes sense. I could almost see what you described. You think I'll be okay?"

"If you follow through on getting the help you need, I think you'll do fine. There's a health food store down the street. Start there. Stop in and ask if they can recommend someone."

"I will. I certainly do not want to forget my family! Thank you, Jennie. Do you have any cards?"

"Cards?"

"Business cards. I'll hand them out for you."

"Oh, yes, I do. Right this way," I said and led her to the front counter where I handed her a few cards.

"Give me more than that, I know a lot of people."

"Thank you, JD," I said.

"No, thank you, Jennie. I really mean it."

As we spoke, Megan was at the counter carefully wrapping a crystal angel with paper. She placed the item in a Sunflowers bag and handed it to the customer along with her receipt.

"Thank you, Ms. Benson," she said, but the woman wasn't paying attention to Megan. She was listening to me and JD, and after JD took additional cards, the woman grabbed one too.

After both women left the store, I asked Megan, "Who was that?"

Megan looked at the receipt. "Her name is Hanna Benson."

"Has she been in here before?"

"I don't think so, why?"

"I just get a feeling I'll be seeing her again," I said.

Megan looked out the window as Hanna drove away, then looked back at me and said, "Okay, if you say so. By the way, Jennie, I had another idea."

I smiled at Megan. "I'm all ears."

"I'd like to design a flier that we can put in the shopping bags. It should list the items we carry in stock, information about readings, and list any upcoming workshops. I could also create your website."

"Wow, Megan! I had no idea you had so many talents. That all sounds great!"

"Yes, and I'm getting to put into practice what I'm learning in my art and business classes. I'll draft a flier and the website. Can we meet about it tomorrow?"

"Yes," I said.

"Okay, but you need to decide the topic of your first seminar."

I flinched as I hadn't planned it yet. I glanced at my watch and said, "Don't you need to leave for school?"

# CHAPTER TWENTY-THREE

## *November*

NOVEMBER HAD ARRIVED, and it was the morning of Evan's birthday party. Jake promptly picked me up and carried my wrapped present, a telescope, out to his Jeep.

As he drove us to the park, he asked, "Who will I be meeting at the party?"

"There's my ex-husband Ben and his wife Jasmine. You'll meet Evan the birthday boy, his older sister Lola, my daughter Kate and her husband Brad. You will also meet my friend Deanna. Other than that, there will be about ten three year olds and their parents, most of whom I've not yet met either."

"That's a lot of three year olds."

"Yes, well, they all go to school with Evan. Kate told me it's been a busy year for parties as the parents invite all the classmates to each one. So far this year, Evan's been to five."

"Sounds like Evan has quite an active social life," Jake said with a laugh. "He'll probably get a lot of gifts today."

"I imagine so. Wait till you see how excited he gets when he's handed a gift. His eyes light up and he shivers with excitement. But what really amazes me for his age, is how grateful he is. He always says thank you without his mother reminding him."

"He sounds like a happy kid."

"Oh, he is."

"It also sounds like you are one of his biggest fans."

"Yes, I am, without a doubt. He stole my heart the minute he was born. All my grandchildren have."

"So you don't have a favorite?"

"No, I don't. I love them all equally, and appreciate their different personalities and traits."

As Jake pulled into the park, we spotted what must be the pavilion. It was decorated with streamers and balloons and lots of children running around. "I guess this is the place," Jake said as he parked the Jeep.

Jake grabbed our gifts from the Jeep and carried them as we walked toward the pavilion. "Here goes," I said.

"You sound nervous," he said.

"I'm always a bit on edge around the family, I guess. You know, family dynamics."

"I understand. You'll be fine. I got your back, and a lovely back it is," he said and smiled at me.

I stopped walking and smiled. "Why thank you, Jake," I said. Jake may have just also stolen my heart.

As Jake and I neared the pavilion, Evan spotted us and yelled, "Nana's here!" He ran to me with open arms and I leaned down to hug him. He kissed my cheek then said, "You're here for my party?"

"Yes, I am."

"Who's that?" he asked as he pointed at Jake.

"That is my friend, Jake."

"Hi, Jake," Evan said. "It's my birthday."

"So I've heard," Jake said.

Evan ran off to play with friends as we walked over to the designated gift table. As Jake placed our gifts on the table, I noticed how tall his gift was. "Golf clubs?" I asked.

"You have to ask? Don't give away the surprise."

I heard, "Hello, Mother," and turned to see Kate.

"Hi, Kate," I said as we hugged. I introduced her to Jake. "This is my friend, Jake Walker."

Kate smiled at him and said, "Nice to meet you." Then she turned toward me and whispered, "Good looking bird you got there, Busy Bee."

I laughed, then blushed. Jake looked at me and asked, "What was that about?"

"I'll tell you later."

Brad walked up to greet us and we made introductions. "Nice to meet you. There's wine and beer in that cooler," Brad said as he pointed at three coolers. "There's ice in the middle one and soda and water in the last one. Please, help yourselves." Brad then walked away to speak with some of his friends.

Kate said, "Daddy and Jasmine are here."

I looked around. "Where?"

"They took Lola to the swings. They should be back soon," she said, then walked away to greet other guests.

"You want a drink?" I asked Jake.

"I guess I'll have a soda."

"You want anything stronger?"

Jake looked at me. "Why? Do you?"

"Maybe."

Jake walked over to the drink coolers and brought me back a chilled and fruity wine cooler. He twisted off the cap, handed me the bottle, and popped the tab on his ginger ale.

"Hi, Nana." I turned at the sound of Lola's voice and watched as she dropped Grandpa Ben and Jasmine's hands and ran toward us. Lola wore a dress trimmed in white lace, ribbons in her hair and had sparkles on her cheeks.

"Hi Lola," I said as she hugged me. "You have fun at the swings with your grandpa and Jasmine?"

"Yes," she said with a nod and a smile.

"That's good. Lola, I'd like you to meet my friend Jake."

"Hi," she said as she shyly gazed up at him.

"I like your sparkles," Jake said.

Lola touched her cheeks as if just remembering the sparkles were there. She pointed at Jasmine and said, "She did it."

"Well, you look lovely," I said. Lola nodded and ran off to play.

"She's a beautiful girl," Jake said. "She takes after her grandmother."

"Thanks, Jake," I said and patted his arm, "that's sweet of you to say. As you can see, Lola is quite shy, especially compared to Evan."

"What did I do?" Jasmine asked as she and Ben walked up to us.

"What are you talking about?" I asked.

"Why was Lola pointing at me? What was she saying?"

"Oh, she said you put the sparkles on her cheeks."

"Oh that," she said with a laugh. "I had promised her the sparkles the last time we visited. It's a good thing I remembered because she had not forgotten."

"Well, she looks adorable," I said.

"And who is this?" Ben asked as he eyed Jake.

"Oh, excuse my manners," I said. "Ben and Jasmine Malone this is Jake Walker."

Ben and Jake shook hands as they sized each other up.

"What do you do, Jake?" Ben asked.

"I work at the Del Vista Pro Shop," he said. "You golf?"

"I did years ago. I wouldn't mind giving it another go sometime."

"Well, anytime you and Jasmine want to try it, let me know and I'll get you the family discount."

"Thanks, Jake. That's generous of you," Ben said.

Our small group stood uncomfortably as we wondered what else to talk about. I was relieved to see Deanna enter the pavilion carrying a gift.

"I'd like you to meet my friend," I said to Jake as I took his hand and pulled him toward her.

# CHAPTER TWENTY-FOUR

I GREETED DEANNA, and introduced her to Jake. "Nice to meet you, Jake," she said.

"Deanna used to work as a medium at Sunflowers," I said.

"Used to? What happened?" he asked.

"Deanna discovered that she didn't like giving readings."

"No, not at all," she said.

"So how are you doing?" I asked her.

"I am loving my work," she said.

"What is it you do?" Jake asked.

"I'm working cold case files," she said. "Both missing persons and crime cases, offering fresh clues."

Jake nodded. "That sounds interesting."

"Oh, it is," she said, "and I don't have to talk to any clients. I work alone and behind the scenes."

Jake looked puzzled. "If you don't meet with people, how do you do what you do?"

"The case manager sends me an email about each case. It contains a fact summary, the age of the missing person or victim along with their description and photo."

"How do you use the information they send you?" I asked.

"I don't read any of it at first. When I receive the email, I print out the person's picture and focus on it. While connected to spirit, I ask for details. Is this person alive? If yes, where is he? If no, where are his remains? Things like that. Then I ask, what happened to this person? I write down everything I receive. After that, I read the summary to see if I can offer more insight. Once I'm done, I email my report to the case manager."

"Have you worked many cases?" Jake asked.

"Yes, and my most recent cold case was about a missing girl. Her school bus driver was the last person to see her. The family lived out in the country and she had to walk a long desolate road to and from the bus stop. In a vision, I saw her running from someone and dropping her doll as she ran. I told the police the doll was in the woods near the road. They found it where I described, under layers of leaves. Her mother later confirmed it was the doll her daughter had taken to school that day."

"Good confirmation," I said.

"But what happened to the missing girl?" Jake asked.

Deanna's eyes saddened. "That's the hard part of what I do. I had a vision of where to find her; and they found her body near there. But I felt such sorrow that it was her remains they found, and not her."

"But you gave her family closure," I said.

"Yes, but it's not over. The case manager said that trace evidence was found, and I gave a description of a man to the sketch artist. I hope they find who did this to her. I prefer the cases that find the person alive and well."

"If they are alive and well why don't they just go home?" Jake asked.

"There are many reasons," Deanna said. "The child may not remember his family, or believes his captors when they say his family doesn't want him back. Or the person may have deliberately run away and not want to be found."

"So are all your cases cold cases?" Jake asked.

"When I first started I was only given older cases. But when my success rate caught the attention of my manager, she added my name to the active case contact list at the police department. I received a current case file this morning. I hope it'll have a happier outcome," Deanna said. "I also work cases with private investigators."

"But by helping to solve cases, aren't you concerned that you'll be called to speak at a trial? Would you be comfortable doing that?" I said.

Deanna shrugged. "I worried about testifying and asked my case manager about it. She said that a prosecutor is not likely to call on a psychic as an expert at a trial."

"Well, that's good," I said.

"Yes, and it sounds like you enjoy what you do," Jake said.

Deanna brightened. "It's very rewarding and I like that I'm using my Gifts to help people, without having to meet with them."

Lola walked up to me and took my hand. "Come here, Nana, I want to show you something," she said and pulled me away from Jake and Deanna. At the center table, Lola pointed at Evan's birthday cake. It was decorated with plastic palm trees, a pirate ship and a pirate chest. The blue and tan icing resembled a sandy beach near blue water.

"Isn't that something, Nana?"

"Yes, it sure is," I said.

"Evan says he's a pirate," she said.

"He does?"

"Yes, but he's not a pirate, right Nana?"

"No, it's just pretend."

Lola smiled, then hugged me and ran off to play. I looked over at Deanna and Jake. What were they talking about?

Deanna walked over to Kate and I sat next to Jake. "What were you two talking about?"

"You first," he said and nodded toward Lola.

"She showed me Evan's birthday cake and asked if her brother was a real pirate."

Jake laughed. "What did you tell her?"

"I said it was pretend. Okay, your turn."

"Okay. Deanna said you were a great friend and an amazing woman."

"She did?"

"Yes, and I agreed with her."

"You did?"

"Yes, I did."

"I wonder why she said that."

"Something about your might needing support, you know, with the family. I assured her you could count on me."

I smile. "Good to know. Thanks."

Kate clapped her hands to get everyone's attention. "The burgers and hot dogs are ready," she said and pointed at the grill where Brad and a friend stood cooking. "Rolls, salads and sides are on this table. Please help yourselves."

Jake and I watched with amusement as the children stampeded toward the food followed by their frenzied parents. The pavilion was abuzz with activity. Jake and I laughed at the chaos, when I realized Ben and Jasmine were laughing with us.

"How is your store doing?" Jasmine asked.

If Ben had asked that question, I'd suspect sarcasm, but not from Jasmine. "It's going great, thanks for asking."

"I've been meaning to stop in. I'll drive over sometime," she said.

"Let me know when so I can be free to show you around the place."

Ben shook his head no. She ignored him and said, "Yes, and maybe we'll go to lunch, too."

# CHAPTER TWENTY-FIVE

WE PILED FOOD on our plates and sat at a table with Deanna. Brad came over and joined us. "It's a good turnout," he said.

I nodded at the overflowing gifts on the center table, and said, "Evan better start opening his gifts soon or we'll be here all night."

Brad laughed, "You may be right. It looks like he won't need any gifts for Christmas."

"Oh, I'm sure there will be something he'll want by then."

"Always is," he said, then turned serious. "I wanted to talk to you about something, Jennie."

"Oh? What is it?"

"It's about Kate."

"What about her?"

"I'm sorry she hasn't come to your store. I've told her she should check it out and give you moral support, but you know how stubborn she can be. She doesn't even want to talk about it."

Jake said, "Doesn't Kate realize all her mother does?"

"Yea, she talks to dead people," Brad said with a laugh.

"It's important work," Jake said. "She helps her clients get answers and receive important messages."

"You a client?" Brad asked.

"I'm a fan," Jake said.

"Thanks, Jake," I said. "Look, Brad, don't push her on it. I wish she'd come over and see it, but I don't want to force her. I just wish I could understand why she was treating me this way."

Brad looked at me with surprise. "You're a medium and you don't know why?"

I blushed. "I seem to have a harder time getting my own answers when I'm emotionally attached to the outcome."

Brad chewed his food a moment, and said, "She's afraid."

"Afraid of what?"

"Afraid you'll get into her head."

"What do you mean?"

"That you'll read her mind. She doesn't want you digging around in her private life."

"I'm not a mind reader and I wouldn't do that," I said. "I don't intrude on people's privacy."

Brad shrugged. "She doesn't see it that way."

"And how do you see it, Brad? What do you think about it?" I asked.

"If it's helpful to your clients, it's a good thing. I've never had ghostly visions or the desire to dabble in the occult. But I once had an interesting dream about talking to my grandfather. I understand that some people are full of questions, especially when it comes to life after death. I'm not sure anyone knows for certain, but if there is life after death, then you are providing a good service."

"Well, thanks, Brad," I said. "But I'd like to point out that the word *occult* means *hidden.*"

Brad nodded as Kate called to him. "We'll have to talk about it later; I'm needed at the grill," he said, and rushed away.

I sipped my wine and said, "Why is family so complicated?"

"You ever hear the story about the guy who left town and became famous?" Jake asked.

"Not sure, tell me," I said.

"The guy became a multimillionaire, but when he went to his class reunion no one in his home town believed he had become a success. They still saw him as the kid who picked his nose and acted like a goof off in school. They could only see him as the kid he had been."

"I'll have you know I've never picked my nose," I said.

"That may be true, but I think you get my point."

I finished my wine and was about to go get another bottle, when Deanna pulled at my sleeve and held me in my seat. "Slow down girl, you'll only regret it."

Jake looked surprised. "Regret what?"

"Keep your head, Jennie. Don't drink too much," she said. "You don't want to say anything you'll regret tomorrow."

Jake was about to comment, as I stood up and said, "No need for concern; Deanna's right." I walked over to the cooler for a bottled water and watched Kate laughing with her dad, Jasmine, and some friends. Why did I care what they thought of me and my career?

As I returned to my seat, I interrupted Deanna. "What were you telling him?"

"I was telling Jake that you feel judged by your family and don't deal very well with it."

I shrugged. "I guess that's because I was raised to be a pleaser, to put every one else's happiness above my own. It hurts when no one cares if I'm happy."

"I care," Jake said.

"Ah, isn't that sweet? Thanks for liking poor little me."

"Stop it, Jennie! That's your ego talking," Deanna said. "When you are living from your higher self you don't feel judged. And you know that our thoughts create our life. So is that what you want to be? You want to be poor?"

"No! And thanks for snapping me out of my mental drama."

Kate clapped her hands again and got everyone's attention. "It's time to sing *Happy Birthday* to our birthday boy," she said as she walked with Evan to the cake table. Kate helped Evan stand on the bench where he could get a better view of the cake. His eyes gleamed with happiness as Brad lit the candles.

We all stood around the table and sang to Evan who smiled and clapped with joy. Kate asked me to help her cut the cake and I volunteered Deanna to scoop the ice cream. After we served everyone, I brought a plate to Jake.

"See?" he said with a smile. "This is why I brought a gift."

"Oh? That's the reason?" Deanna asked as she sat at our table.

"Yes," Jake said, "you have to bring a gift if you want cake and ice cream."

We all watched Evan open his gifts. With each present, his eyes would widen with joy. After opening each present, he'd say a sincere thank you.

Evan opened Jake's gift last. He pulled a golf club and a golf ball from the golf bag and walked over to the grass. Evan placed the ball on the ground and struck it with the club.

"The kid's a natural!" Jake said.

# CHAPTER TWENTY-SIX

THE PARTY HAD been great fun, and the busy parents were now gathering and ushering their children to their cars. Jake and I said goodbye to Deanna, Ben and Jasmine, then got busy helping Kate and Brad clean the pavilion.

Jake helped Brad pull the decorations from the rafters while Kate and I tossed empty plates and cups into a trash bag.

"He seems nice," Kate said with a nod toward Jake.

"Yes, he's very nice," I said as I grabbed another trash bag.

"How long have you known him?"

"We met a few weeks ago."

"Why didn't you tell me?"

I shrugged. "I didn't think you'd care."

"Of course I do. You're my mother. Does he work?"

"He manages the Del Vista golf shop."

"Oh? You don't golf, so where did you meet?"

"At my store."

"Oh," she said.

Again with the silent treatment? No more questions? Guess that was the end of the discussion. We cleaned the tables, packed the food into the coolers and helped load

Evan's presents into their car. Everything was clean and done when I walked over to my daughter and said, "Kate?"

"Yes?"

"Why won't you come to my store?"

She shrugged.

"I sense that you're afraid of my intruding in your life."

Silence.

"I won't do that. I promise to not use my Gifts to dig into your privacy."

"But you just said that you sense why I won't come to the store."

"Yes."

"Well, doesn't sensing mean that you're reading me and my life?"

Kate's words stung. And she twisted my words and shoved them back down my throat. As I choked on them, I felt a sharp pain in my gut. Tears swelled in my eyes. I had always wanted nothing but the best for her and her family, and to be a part of it. But I also wanted, no needed, to live my Gifts and help people. Why did it have to be one or the other? Why couldn't it be all the above?

I walked over to Evan, knelt down and hugged him. "Nana loves you," I said with tears in my eyes.

"Why are you crying, Nana?" he asked.

I wiped away my tears. "I'm just happy to see you."

"Then why do you look sad?" Lola asked as she ran up to us.

"I'm just sad to say goodbye."

"Oh," Lola said.

Evan mimicked her with another, "Oh."

I hugged the children to me.

"Why do you have to?" Lola asked.

"Why do I have to what, Lola?"

"Why do you have to say goodbye?"

"Because I'm going home now."

"Can we come with you?"

I looked at their mother, who stood with her arms folded across her chest, watching us.

"I'd like that sometime," I said, speaking loud enough for Kate to hear.

Lola ran up to her mother. "Can we stay with Nana?"

"No, not tonight," Kate said.

"When can we?" Lola said.

"I don't know," Kate said.

I hugged Evan to me, not wanting to ever let him go. He was my darling little man, and he was growing up so fast. I wished I could see him and Lola and Emily more often.

He hugged into me, and said, "Thank you for coming to my party, Nana." Then ran to his father who was pushing the new bike to the car. "Wait, Daddy, I want to ride it."

Evan climbed on the bike and balanced on the seat as he grabbed the handle bars. He placed his feet on the pedals and said, "I'm ready." Brad pulled the bike a few feet, and Evan's eyes grew wide. "Help me, Daddy, I'm scared!" Evan said as he pointed to the slope ahead. It must have looked quite high to the child, but an adult would barely notice.

"I got you, Buddy," Brad said.

Kate took Lola's hand and pulled her to the car. My granddaughter looked back at me, blew me a kiss, and said, "Bye, Nana."

I blew a kiss to her as Kate opened the car door and helped Lola into her car seat. Then without a glance my way or a word of goodbye, Kate got into the passenger seat and shut the door.

The vision burned in my mind and my emotions swelled within me. I stood there unable to speak or move as Brad lifted Evan off the bike and helped him into his car seat. Brad put the bike in the back of the car, turned and waved at us, and got in the car and drove away.

My heart ached. Every family goodbye was painful. Each time my heart felt like it would break in two. But Kate's icy goodbye hurt at my core. What has to happen to dissolve this wedge in our relationship? Teary eyed, I stood staring at the empty space where their car had been. It took a moment to realize that Jake's hand was on my shoulder.

"Are you okay?" he asked.

I shook my head as I wiped my tears and turned toward him. "What good are my Gifts if I have to choose them over my family?" I hugged him, my head on his shoulder as I cried.

We sat on a bench and I said, "Why is it that those we love the most, hurt us the deepest?"

He hugged me and said, "I promise to never hurt you, Jen."

His words were like a warm balm. It was the first time that Jake had made any hint of love and I valued that. But as much as I cherished Jake and his thoughtfulness, my heart was following the car that carried Brad, Kate, Lola and Evan home.

Jake and I walked to his Jeep in silence. He opened the door, and I slid onto the leather seat. He walked around to the driver's side and got in. I expected him to drive after starting the engine, but instead he turned to look at me.

"Don't give anyone the power to distinguish your Gifts."

"What do you mean?"

"You can't live your life for your kids. You can't not do what you do to make Kate happy."

"Thanks. I guess I needed to hear that. It just puzzles me that my Gifts help other families, but not my own."

Jake nodded. "Give her time, she'll come around. In the meantime, you are offering a great service to your clients."

"Thank you. I appreciate your saying that."

"And there's something I've wanted to ask you."

"What is it?"

"I have to go up and check on the cabin over Thanksgiving weekend. Would you go with me?"

Even with Kate's silent treatment and all the drama, time with my grandchildren was what I cherished most. But Jake was offering me the opportunity to get away for a while, and have some me time. "Yes, I'll go with you. I'd like that."

He smiled. "I was afraid you'd say no because of the family."

"A trip to the mountains may be just what I need."

# CHAPTER TWENTY-SEVEN

THE FARONIS SAT across from me at my reading table on this chilly November morning. The grief stricken faces of both the man and his wife made it obvious they had recently lost someone dear.

"Our daughter overdosed," the woman said. "She was at a dance and a guy dropped a drug in her drink."

"They told us she didn't suffer," her husband said. "Is our daughter okay?"

I sensed their daughter's presence in the room with us. She was eager to start the reading. I closed my eyes and connected with spirit. When I opened my eyes, I felt drawn into a vision. There was a blur of activity then I felt a sharp bump on the back of my head. She must have bumped her head when she passed out. There was a quick release as her spirit left her body. I shared the vision with the couple.

"So she didn't suffer?" he said.

"No, it happened quickly," I said.

"I'm relieved to hear that," he said.

"Did she like her funeral?" Mrs. Faroni asked.

I cringed at the question. I don't care for funerals as I find them to be morbid. The casket at the front of the room, the body no longer animated by its spirit. My father had a funeral, but my mother had a service instead. I preferred the memorial service, with lots of flowers and a display of photographs celebrating her life. It was a better way to remember a loved one in my opinion. But I had to put my thoughts aside as I silently asked their daughter if she liked her funeral.

In a flash, I saw a vision of the young woman's body in a casket surrounded by flowers. I repeated what I received to the couple. "Your daughter was at the funeral. She says all the flowers were lovely, but she is sorry to see you still so sad. She knows you miss her, and she wants you to know she is okay."

Mr. Faroni said, "I never thought I'd see a medium. But at her funeral it felt like my daughter wasn't in the casket. Her body was there, but not her personality. So if she wasn't in there, where was she?"

The young woman appeared by her father, and I said, "She is standing next to you."

He looked startled as he looked around the room. "She is?"

"Yes, her hand is on your shoulder, and she is asking you to take care of Pipe in. Pip in?"

He smiled. "It's Pippin. That's her poodle. I've been wondering about taking the dog to the pound. My wife here thinks it's crazy. It acts like it's seeing things."

"He is. He is seeing your daughter," I said. "He sees her spirit."

Mrs. Faroni looked surprised. "Really?"

"Yes," I said. "Some animals seem more attuned to seeing spirit. I have a friend who has three dogs, but only one seems to see spirits. The other two either can't see the spirits or ignores them. She's not sure which."

"If that's the case," Mrs. Faroni said, "then Pippin stays with us."

The young woman smiled at her mother, and I said, "Your daughter's delighted to hear that."

"Is there anything else?" her father asked. "Anything she wants to tell us?"

"Yes, she wants you to remember the good memories. She wants you to know that she didn't suffer. She wants you to let the courts take care of the guy and to stop hating him. She understands why you are angry with him, but the resentment is hurting you. He suffers too, and it was a horrible accident."

"An accident? He gave my daughter a drug in the hopes of defiling her, which was bad enough, but instead he killed her! You're saying I'm supposed to forgive him? I don't think so! That schmuck should burn in hell for what he did," Mr. Faroni said.

I'd be furious too if someone had taken my daughter's life. But this was not about me, so I dropped that line of thinking to reconnect to spirit.

"She had her whole life ahead of her," Mrs. Faroni said.

"She still does," I said. "She is still alive and living her spiritual path. You can sense her, can't you?"

"Yes, I think I do," she said as her husband nodded in agreement.

"Know that she is okay. She is alive and well and is still living her life... just not here."

# CHAPTER TWENTY-EIGHT

IT WAS THANKSGIVING Eve and Jake was driving us north on I-75. The ride had been flat and monotonous until we got north of Atlanta where Jake exited onto the Appalachian Highway. We traveled north through beautiful rolling hills, and past small towns with unusual names like Jasper, Talking Rock and Ellijay. We climbed higher in elevation as we entered the mountains of northern Georgia.

"There really are mountains in north Georgia. You weren't kidding," I said.

"No, I wasn't. It surprises most people."

Jake turned off the main highway in the town of Blue Ridge and parked in front of Mercier Orchards. We entered the store and ate lunch in the deli. After lunch we explored the store and sampled apples, salsas and jams. We selected a jar of Vidalia Onion Georgia Peach hot sauce, a bag of Cameo apples and a jar of Bunch O'Berries jam.

"This place is wonderfully delicious," I said as I nibbled on a crisp apple while we walked back to the Jeep.

Near where we parked, there was a display of hand carved wood sculptures of bears, eagles and turtles. We walked closer to watch the carver work a block of wood. A display sign next to him said he was currently carving a raccoon.

"I like your work," I said.

He looked at us and said, "Thanks."

"Would you like to have one of those carvings?" Jake asked.

"I would, but I have no place to put it," I said.

"Well, maybe someday you will," he said.

I shrugged, and looked at him with curiosity. What was he implying?

Once back in the Jeep, Jake headed north from Blue Ridge. We drove past the towns of Morganton and Blairsville. In Young Harris we climbed higher, and then drove down a deep incline into the town of Hiawassee. Or what I would have named the place... Paradise.

I was in awe as I looked out at the mountains that seemed to rise up out of the lake. My mouth must have dropped open, for Jake looked at me and laughed, then said, "You like it?"

"Oh, yes."

"That's Lake Chatuge, which I think of as Lake Tahoe East," he said as he turned off the main highway and drove down a country lane that led to his family's cabin.

But this cabin was not the quaint little cottage I had imagined. It was a wood and stone house on a large and sloped lakefront lot.

Jake parked in the driveway, then we got out and stretched as we looked at the long range view of Lake Chatuge. Jake stood behind me as he pointed at the mountains in the distance. "Those mountains are in North Carolina."

"You can see all the way to North Carolina from here?"

"Yes," he said. "Lake Chatuge is in both Georgia and North Carolina. If we get in a boat ride this weekend, I'll show you the buoys that mark the state line."

I laughed, "You're kidding, right?"

"No, the lake is about half in each state. And the dam is at the northern rim in North Carolina."

"There's a dam, too?"

"Yes, this is a TVA lake."

"What does that mean?"

"It's one of the lakes controlled by the Tennessee Valley Authority. Back in the 1940s the TVA built the dam to flood the Hiwassee River, which is spelled different than the Georgia town. As the river expanded into this lake, it covered thousands of acres of land."

"Why did they do it?"

"To bring the electricity generated by the TVA dams to the region."

"Well, the TVA created a beautiful lake."

We pulled our bags and suitcases from the Jeep and carried them to the front door. The front of the house was faced with river rock and stone and the front door contained an intricate beveled glass design.

Jake unlocked the door and said, "Come on in and I'll give you the tour."

I followed him into the house and waited on the tiled entryway as Jake walked across the living room. He pulled a drapery cord revealing a windowed wall with a panoramic view of the lake. It was enchanting!

"You can leave your things here for now," he said as he took my hand. "Let me show you around."

He showed me the dining room, the kitchen and the laundry room. Then we walked downstairs where Jake showed me the small kitchenette, a fireplace and two guest room suites. "My folks had intended to rent out the downstairs, but they never did," he said.

Back upstairs Jake showed me the library-music area off to one side of the living room. Books crammed the bookcases, and several guitars and an amp rested on the floor. Jake lifted an acoustic guitar from a stand and strummed it.

"Been a while since I've played," he said as he tuned the guitar. "I'm a bit out of practice," he said and played a chain of songs.

I listened, delighted by his musical talent. As he put the guitar back in its stand, I said, "That was awesome!"

He shrugged and smiled at me. "Glad you liked it."

Jake led me up to the master suite. There was a king size bed, two large walk-in closets and a lakefront view.

The master bath had two sinks, a shower and a Jacuzzi tub.

"Well, what do you think of the place?"

Was I ready for this? I gazed at Jake. Oh yes, I am ready. Jake was so kind and handsome. The house was lovely, the views breathtaking. It was all so much more than I had expected. "This is some cabin," I said.

"I hope you'll be comfortable here."

"Oh, I think I'll manage," I said with a laugh.

"You can put your things in here," he said as he pointed at the dresser. "I have to go outside and turn on the water and check on a few things. Make yourself at home."

While Jake was outside, I unpacked my suitcase, hung my clothes in the closet and folded the rest into a dresser drawer. I slid the empty suitcase under the bed then walked back to the living room.

I opened the back door and stepped out onto the porch. The sights and sounds of the mountain lake was captivating. As if on cue, a flock of geese flew by in formation, gliding along the surface of the lake. It was all so magical.

I sat on the porch swing and closed my eyes as I took in the sounds of nature. I opened my eyes and meditated on the magnificent view before me. "Thank you, God," I whispered, "for this beauty, for this trip and for bringing Jake into my life."

Then my thoughts turned toward Connie. This was their place.

*'What does she think about my being here?'* I asked my guides.

"Connie is happy for you both... have no fear," Mica said. "It's okay to feel contentment."

"Enjoying the view?" Jake asked, startling me.

"Yes, I am."

"The temperature's dropping, so you might want to enjoy the view from inside the house."

The sky had cast its rosy glow on the trees and the surface of the lake. There was a chill in the air as Jake held out his hand. I took it and stepped from the swing. He pulled me to him and kissed me. I hugged into him, my head on his chest, listening to his heart and smelling his cologne. He exuded warmth, safety and virility. I gazed into his eyes and melted as we kissed. Our lips lingered as he pulled me even closer. Basking in his warmth, I no longer cared if the temperature was dropping.

"Come inside," Jake said.

# CHAPTER TWENTY-NINE

AS WE STEPPED into the living room, I saw that Jake had lit the fireplace. "Have a seat," he said, "I'll be right back."

I sat on the sofa, slipped off my shoes and enjoyed the warmth from the fire on my feet and hands. Jake returned and set a tray on the coffee table. It contained two wine glasses, a bottle of Riesling and a plate of crackers, cheese and apple slices.

"Did you have all this in the cooler?" I said, surprised by all the food.

"No, I phoned my neighbors the other day and asked them to stock a few things. Stan and his wife, Margot, knew my parents and have been keeping an eye on this place for me."

"Well, it's a blessing to have good neighbors."

"Yes, it is. They invited us to join them for Thanksgiving dinner. I told them we had other plans, but would stop in for a visit this weekend."

I was glad to hear we wouldn't be dining with them. I understood why he felt obligated to visit with them, but I hoped to have Jake all to myself.

"We can make a stir fry for dinner tonight," Jake said. "And tomorrow, we'll feast on some turkey with all the trimmings. And if the weather's warm enough we'll take a ride on the lake."

"That would be wonderful. I'd love a boat ride."

Jake nodded. "On Friday, we can hike to some waterfalls and on Saturday I'll show you Brasstown Bald."

"What's Brasstown Bald?"

"It's the highest peak in Georgia, over 4,700 feet above sea level. The observation deck there has a great view of the lake and mountains. And if the weather's clear we'll be able to see as far as the tallest buildings in Atlanta. After that we can dine in Helen, that is if you like German food."

"Yes, I do."

"There are other good restaurants there, but I'm partial to the sauerbraten," he said, and took a sip of wine. "I hope you don't mind my making plans."

I smiled. "No, whatever you want to do is fine," I said, just as long as I'm with you.

He put his wine glass on the table, and leaned toward me. "I like making you happy, Jen."

I set my glass on the table and leaned closer to him. "I like that, too," I said. We kissed, and lingered, enjoying the connection. We sat closer and Jake put his arm around my shoulders. I nestled into him as we gazed at the fire.

"Is it too soon to say I love you?" he said.

I blushed. "No, I love you too."

He stood up and pulled me to him. "Let me show you how much," he said, and led me to his bedroom.

I sat on the edge of his bed, nervous that this moment had come. He sat next to me, and when we kissed, I melted into him. I wanted him, too. We laid on the bed kissing, hugging and exploring each other. Jake was unbuttoning my blouse, when I stopped him. Was Connie here? Could I sense her in the room? I should know better. The individual known as Connie was no more, and her spirit had assured me she was happy I was with Jake. The fear had been a gut reaction, and I pushed it from my mind. But as we kissed, another anxious thought popped up. I'm no longer young, will he find me attractive?

Jake pulled away and looked at me. "What's wrong?"

"It's been a long time, and I don't want to disappoint you."

"Have no fear, it's been a long time for me, too."

"You're joking."

"No, I'm not."

"Well, I'm not twenty years old anymore."

Jake laughed. "Neither am I, so relax," he said. We stood up, and I helped him fold the quilt to the foot of the bed. Jake removed his shirt and pants and I admired his still muscular physique for his age. My eyes dropped to the hairline that trailed from his belly button down into his briefs. It was, in my opinion, one of the sexiest parts on a man.

I pulled off my jeans and unbuttoned my shirt, but kept it on as we laid on the sheets. We kissed and caressed.

Jake pulled off my shirt and unhooked my bra. He smiled and kissed my lips, my neck, my breasts...

I quivered with anticipation. It had been a long time since I'd been with a man, and no man had ever made me feel as good as Jake did. He kissed my belly and reached into my panties. When his fingers touched in me, I gasped.

Jake removed his jockeys, and I blushed at how well-endowed and ready he was. I kissed him from head to toe, then he kissed me from my toes and lingered between my thighs, teasing and taunting me. I groaned as lights flashed in my mind. I held to the feeling as long as I could, then quivered with release. Yes, this man was electrifying!

He entered slowly, then at a faster rhythm. He gazed in my eyes as I fell into his again. Who was this man? Why had I fallen for him so hard, so fast? Was he my soul mate?

His skin dimpled and his nipples grew hard as he finished. He rolled over and laid on his back. I rolled onto my side, under his arm with my head on his chest. His heart was beating fast as he kissed the top of my head.

He pulled the quilt around us and as we cuddled, I fell into a deep sleep. I dreamt of geese gliding in formation, and of me flying over the surface of the lake with them.

☼

Jake stirred and woke me. I looked at the clock and said, "You hungry?"

"For you? Yes," he said and hugged me to him.

"I meant for dinner," I said with a giggle.

"Oh, yes, that, too," he said.

We took a shower together, but as I rinsed off, Jake slid in from behind. We came at the same time, and I said, "You're going to get me pregnant!"

"Is that possible?"

"No," I said.

"Cause that would be okay with me."

"Not me! At my age I'm happy being the grandmother."

"And you are such a beautiful grandmother."

I blushed, then laughed.

"No, I mean it. You turn me on."

As I gazed into his eyes, the passion burning there took my breath away. I kissed him under the streaming shower, then we rinsed each other off. Jake turned off the water and opened the shower door. He grabbed a bath towel from the cabinet and bundled me in it. "Don't you catch a chill," he said.

I thanked him as he leaned out for a second towel. We dried off and slipped on comfortable clothes.

"You ready for some stir fry?" he asked.

"Yes, I'm famished. Is there dessert, too?"

"Yes," he said, "you."

I laughed, then blushed again in anticipation.

# CHAPTER THIRTY

## *Thanksgiving*

JAKE MADE US a delicious omelet for breakfast. After eating, I went outside and sat on the porch-swing, wrapped in a blanket. I sipped a cup of coffee and gazed out at the lake and mountains. It felt wonderful to be alone here with Jake. I had a lot to be thankful for this Thanksgiving morning.

Jake stepped onto the dock, startling two ducks nestled at the shore. He flipped a switch on a post and the boat lowered into the water. He removed the tarp and climbed aboard to check the engine. He jumped back onto the dock and walked up the path toward the cabin. He climbed the stairs up to the porch and said, "Enjoying the view?"

"I can't get enough of it."

"Well, you haven't seen enough of it, yet. Come on, let's go for a boat ride."

Jake took my coffee cup as I unraveled myself from my blanketed cocoon. "You better put on your heavy coat, gloves and hat," he said. "It's warm in the sun, but the air coming off the water will be cool."

I nodded and went into the house for my coat, hat, gloves, camera, cell phone and two bottled waters. Jake had waited on the porch and when I stepped outside he took my hand and led me down to the dock. As I glanced at the beautiful wood grained boat bobbing on the waves, I noticed the name on the stern was *Let's Go*.

"What a beautiful boat!" I said.

"It's a Chris-Craft," Jake said. "It was my father's boat. I learned to waterski behind it when I was a kid. Do you ski?"

"Not since I was young. Do you still ski?"

"I get on skis a few times each summer, but it does wear on my knees now. Can't do the jumps or the tricks I used to do. Hop in," he said.

I climbed into the front passenger seat and sat down. Jake hopped into the driver's seat and started the engine. It gave a thunderous roar as he idled away from the dock. When we reached the center of the cove, Jake gave the engine full throttle and it surged forward like a race horse leaving the gate.

I pulled my jacket tighter around me. The wind was colder on the water, but the ride was thrilling.

"Are you cold?" Jake yelled over the roar of the engine. "You want to head back?"

I shook my head. "No, this is wonderful," I said. "I haven't been in a powerboat since I was a teenager."

Jake pointed out some landmarks as he steered. It was fun looking at all the small cottages, houses and large mansions nestled in the various coves. There were few boats on the lake. Must be too cold for those who had the luxury of being at the lake all year. Jake pointed to a buoy off to the right and said, "Welcome to North Carolina."

I snapped a picture of the buoy and as Jake rounded a bend, snapped pictures of the dam. He pulled near its shore, and idled back on the throttle. "You want to get out and see it?"

"No, that's okay," I said as I snapped his picture.

Jake throttled forward, steering us in and around the many coves, then passed the buoy again. We were back in Georgia. He motored under a bridge and pulled up to a small island. "This was a graveyard before they flooded the river. Do you want to see the old headstones?"

"Okay."

Jake jumped to the shore and tied the bowline to a tree. He came back to the boat and helped me to the ground. We hiked up the hill to where the old cemetery had been.

I studied the few weathered headstones, then glanced out at the lake. "This must have been high ground before they raised the water level," I said.

"Yes, this would have been a hill looking out at the river."

"How old is this cemetery?"

"From what I've read, this cemetery was on a settler's farm. In 1942, before they flooded the land, they had to relocate hundreds of graves."

Jake and I walked to the top of the steep hill, then down and around the backside and up again to the top. I stood with my eyes closed, imagining how it must have been back then, this cemetery on a high hill overlooking the valley and the river. In what others ways had this land flooding affected the people who had lived here?

The farmland was now a beautiful lake. But it must have been quite an undertaking to clear the valley so it would be safe for swimming and navigation.

"Are you okay?" Jake said. "You look sad."

"Oh, I was just thinking about how flooding the river must have affected the people who lived here."

Jake nodded as a boat full of people rode past the island. The TVA had indeed brought electricity with all its modern conveniences to the area. And fun activities, too.

We walked down the hill and Jake helped me into the boat. He untied it from the tree, and tossed the rope into the boat, then pushed us away from the shore as he jumped in.

Jake steered in and out of the coves as we made our way to the other end of the lake. He pulled back the throttle and said, "You want to drive?"

"No, not today," I said.

He pushed the throttle and smiled at me huddled in my coat. "You're cold?"

"Yes, a little," I said, my teeth chattering.

"Slide over here," he said. "I'll keep you warm."

Jake idled the boat as I slid across the seat to him. He put his arm around me and I hugged into him. He felt so warm and sexy.

"I've shown you about all the lake I can show you in the lowered water levels," he said. "Guess we'll head on home."

"Thanks, Jake. It's been a delightful ride," I said, and enjoyed the views during our ride back to his dock.

# CHAPTER THIRTY-ONE

JAKE DOCKED THE boat and handed me the house key. "Go on in and get warm. I'll be right up," he said as he helped me to the dock. He walked over, picked up the canvas cover and carried it toward the boat.

"Do you want help covering the boat?"

"I appreciate the offer, but if you're cold, I can do it."

I wanted to help him, but I was shivering and needed to get warm. "How about I start dinner?"

"That's sounds good."

As I walked up the path to the house I noticed a man and a woman standing on the porch of the house next door watching me. They waved, and I waved back. Must be the helpful neighbors. I walked up to the porch, unlocked the door and stepped into the living room. A man sitting on the sofa startled me. Who the heck was he? As I approached him I realized the man was from spirit.

"Hello," I said.

He nodded and smiled.

I sat on the sofa near him and looked closer. He had a strong resemblance to Jake. "Are you Jake's father?"

He nodded again.

I closed my eyes and envisioned raising my energy vibration higher to better communicate with him. When I opened my eyes, he was watching me connect.

He smiled at me, and said, "Tell Jake to check the attic for squirrels."

"Squirrels?" I said. Then an image flashed in my mind of an attic and squirrels nesting there. "Okay, I'll tell him."

He nodded. "I'm glad you are enjoying our home. You are most welcomed here," he said, and faded from view.

This was one of those rare occasions where I saw spirit without creating the intention first. How normal this way of life had become.

Jake opened the door and stepped inside, looking surprised to find me in the living room. "The kitchen's in there," he said, pointing toward it.

"Pardon?"

"You said you were going to start dinner."

"Oh! You are right. I did say that, but I got side tracked."

Jake walked up to me and said, "I see that. What's up?"

"We had a visitor."

"Who?"

"I'm quite sure he was your father."

"You spoke with my Dad?"

"Yes."

"Huh," Jake said and sat on the sofa.

"He was sitting right where you are now," I said.

Jake jumped to his feet. "Where is he?"

"He's not here now."

"Why was he here?"

"He had a message for you. He said to check the attic for squirrels."

"Okay, I'll check it. Did he say anything else?"

I blushed. "Yes, he said that he was glad I was enjoying his home and welcomed me here."

Jake smiled. "I'm glad he approves. And it's true."

"What is?"

"You are most welcomed here," he said and kissed me.

Dinner would have to wait.

☼

After all the years of preparing huge Thanksgiving dinners for the family, I enjoyed this quiet meal alone with Jake. We ate in the dining room looking out the windows at the marvelous colors of the day turning into night. The lake and mountains were now hidden under an inky black cloak of darkness.

After dinner, we went to the living room. Jake tossed more wood on the fire, and I got a sense of why he felt so at home here. Who wouldn't in this wonderful place?

"Enjoy your meal?" he asked.

"Yes," I said patting my stomach. "It was delicious, and I am stuffed."

Jake sat next to me on the sofa and we cuddled. I said, "Jake? I was wondering about something, but only if you want to tell me."

"What is it?"

"That day you came to my office for a reading, what answer were you seeking?"

Jake laughed. "It seems funny now."

"Oh? Why's that?"

"Because, at the time, I couldn't decide."

"I still don't know what you are talking about. What was the question?"

He smiled. "You really don't know?"

"No, I guess not."

"It was about this place."

"What about it?"

"Well, after I lost Connie, I spent a great deal of time alone here."

"Did you and Connie spend a lot of time here? I mean before she..."

"No, we visited my folks a few times and we planned to retire here. But Connie and I never got that chance. And while this place holds many fond memories, I didn't know if I wanted to hang onto it."

"Why wouldn't you?"

"Well, don't get me wrong. I like this place, but it can get too quiet by myself."

I looked around the cabin. If I owned this wonderful place, I would never give it up.

"But then I got my answer."

"You did? What was it?"

"The answer was you. I like sharing this place with you."

My heart jumped with joy as I smiled at Jake. "Thank you. I really like it here."

"Yes, I can tell."

Jake's eyes softened. He leaned in for a tender kiss and it felt so good, so right. After being with Ben and Richard I had postponed having another relationship. But it felt safe to fall in love with Jake. It was as if we've loved each other over many lifetimes.

"Why don't we go and get more comfortable," Jake said as he stood up and led me to the bedroom.

I stood by the bed with my back to him as I undressed.

"Turn around. Let me look at you," he said.

When I turned around, he was already in the bed.

"You are so beautiful, Jen."

He meant it! I relaxed as I slid under the covers with him. His hands were warm, his touch tender as we kissed and explored each other. I traced my finger around his strong chest, down his tight abs and lingered at his belly button. He was erect and ready and I quickened as he pulled me toward him. We kissed, then I straddled him as he slid inside. I rode him with a slow pulsating rhythm, then he rolled on top and I paced him. I let go of fear and inhibition and relaxed into being one with him and we released.

He turned me to my side and hugged my back. I had never felt so loved, so cared for, or so sexy. He kissed my neck, and said, "I love you, Jen."

Tears stung my eyes. How was it possible to have loved Jake from the moment we met? And he felt the same way. I turned toward him and said, "I love you, too."

☼

As we got ready for bed, Jake said, "I have an idea for your Christmas gift. I know it's early to bring it up, but it involves planning."

"It does?"

"Yes, and packing."

"Are you talking about taking a trip? I can't. Christmas is about being with family."

"That's the plan."

"It is? What is the gift?"

"Ohio."

"Ohio? What do you mean?"

"I'd like to take you to Ohio to see your granddaughter at Christmas. But only if that's okay with you."

I burst into tears and hugged him. No one had ever given me such a thoughtful gift.

"Does that mean yes?"

"Yes, it does! Thank you."

We cuddled in bed and drifted to sleep.

In my dream, I met with Connie. "I am happy you are with Jake," she said. "He's a good man and needs a good woman."

"I'm glad you approve," I said.

# CHAPTER THIRTY-TWO

THE NEXT MORNING Jake and I sat on the porch swing, sipping our coffee and looking out at the lake. I looked at the forest across the cove and asked, "You ever go camping?"

"Yes, many times. We'll have to go someday."

"Someday," I laughed, "that was Ben's favorite phrase. Someday we'll take a houseboat ride down the river. Someday we'll travel out west. Someday we'll explore Canada. Only with Ben, someday never comes," I said.

I stopped talking. Why was I talking about Ben? "Oh, Jake, I'm so sorry that I mentioned Ben," I said.

Jake said nothing as he stared out at the lake.

"Jake, I'm sensing that you want to ask me something."

"Yes, there is something on my mind. I don't mean to pry, but since you brought him up, I am curious about him."

"You are?"

"Yes, but if you are uncomfortable talking about it, we'll change the subject," Jake said.

*'Why the interest?'* I asked and listened for guidance. "Are you wanting to know what happened between me and Ben so we don't go down the same path?"

"Something like that," Jake said. "I care about you and I'd like to know what happened between you and Ben so we don't repeat it."

I debated what to say as I watched a small bird land on the bird feeder at the far end of the porch. The feeder spun from the bird's weight as it nibbled at the seeds in the suet, then flew away.

I loved Jake, and didn't want to screw it up. We had a good thing, and I sensed something special about him from the moment we met. I sipped my coffee as I wrestled with indecision. What good would it do to talk about Ben? What harm would it do? I weighed my thoughts as if on a scale in my mind, and the scale tipped.

I looked at Jake. "Okay, but I won't bore you with every detail of my marriage; just enough to assure you that we won't fall into the same rabbit hole."

"How can you be so sure?"

"Well, for starters, you and I are not teenagers. At eighteen I got pregnant and married."

"Okay, that's a good point. We are not eighteen," Jake said, and pretended to mark an imaginary score card.

I laughed. "Are you keeping a tally?"

"I guess I am," he said with a laugh, then grew serious. "That point alone is good enough if you are uncomfortable talking about this."

I wanted to ease his concern. "Our relationship's nothing like I had with Ben," I said, and drank the last of my coffee.

Jake took the empty cup from my hand and refilled it from the thermos he had brought outside with us.

"You just added a bonus point in the plus column," I said.

"Why's that?"

"Because you are so thoughtful. Ben would not have refilled my cup without my asking him. And he never held the door open for me, even when I was pregnant. He never did things like that... not for me anyway."

"I'll never take you for granted, Jennie," he said. "I like to anticipate your needs. I like to make you happy."

"Thank you," I said, and dabbed my tears with the sleeve of my sweatshirt as I asked my guides what to tell Jake about Ben.

"Just enough," Mica said.

"Well, after Kate was born, I went back to work. Ben and I both hated our jobs, and he reminded me daily that if I hadn't gotten pregnant he would have gone to college and on to a great career. He resented my getting pregnant and I think he still resents me for it to this day."

"It takes two to make a baby," Jake said.

"Yes, I know. But I was young and raised to be a pleaser. This trait along with my empathic nature made it easy for Ben to feed me guilt. I told Ben I'd help him go to college, and he shocked me by quitting his job! I didn't mind helping, but I assumed we'd both work to pay his tuition. But he said that rather than work, he'd sell his artwork. Only, he never sold any of his paintings.

"I got a better paying job as a bookkeeper for a CPA firm. But soon found out I was pregnant again. I told Ben he had to get full-time income. He got angry, but he got a job at a builders supply. After Nathan was born, I stayed home with both children, happy to at last be a full time mother. But Ben said it wasn't fair."

"Not fair that you were raising his kids?" Jake said, raising an eyebrow.

"No, not fair that I was enjoying myself and he wasn't. He kept piling guilt on me. So I put the kids in daycare and went back to work at the firm." The anger I still felt at the memory surprised me. Hadn't I dealt with my feelings about Ben? Judging the anger and resentment that still simmered in me, I guess I hadn't.

"I resented that I couldn't be the stay at home mom my mother had been. And he refused to help with the kids, was always too busy working or creating art. I'd rush the kids to daycare on my way to work. Rush from work to pick them up. Rush through their meals, bath times and bed times. I felt stressed and depressed that the daycare had better quality time with my children than I had.

"I threw myself at my work, and the firm rewarded my efforts with generous pay raises. With Ben and I both working full-time we were finally saving money and soon bought a house. At last, we had our own home, good paying jobs and were paying off debt. But Ben didn't share my domestic bliss.

"One day he told me that a friend had bought one of his paintings. He told me it was a sign to get back to his art, and that he had given notice to quit work. I wanted to support his dreams, but this turn of events shocked me. I thought we were on the same track, saving for our future and getting out of debt. Instead, I again became the sole support of our lifestyle. But I agreed to give him one year to make a go of it."

"That was a generous offer," Jake said. "And what about your dreams?"

Jake's comments pulled me from the memory stream. I shrugged and said, "At the time my dream was to be a wife and mother. That's all I had wanted."

I sipped my coffee and said, "Ben turned our garage into an art studio. His supplies put a serious dent in our budget and he wasn't selling paintings. I'd point to each painting and ask, 'Why not sell this one? Or that one?' For each painting he'd have a reason not to sell it. Why wouldn't he sell them? Did he fear success? Did he really think they were not good enough? I'm no expert, but I thought they were all good.

"After a few months, Ben attended an art show and sold a few of his paintings, but it wasn't enough. We were deep in debt. Ben said to give it one more week, which led to several more months. Then one night, unable to sleep, I stared up at the bedroom ceiling, calculating the credit card debts. I doubted I'd ever pay them off."

"That was a lot of stress for you to shoulder alone," Jake said. "He was your husband and partner."

"Ben was oblivious to any of that. He was an artiste and didn't want to bother with finances. Finally, I had enough. I told him that he had to go back to work and paint on the side. He got furious and said it was my fault he hadn't succeeded. He'd rant at me in front of our children. It didn't affect Nathan, but Kate still sees me as the bad guy. It was my fault her daddy was unhappy, and I'm the one who broke up her happy home."

"That's unfortunate," Jake said.

I looked at Jake, feeling vulnerable and exposed.

Jake took my hand and squeezed it. "I'm sorry you went through all that, Jen. You're not a bad person in my eyes."

"Thank you. Should I continue?"

"I'm here to listen, if you need to talk."

I've never talked about the marriage to anyone before. Perhaps I needed to get the poisoned emotions out before I could let Jake's love in.

I sighed, then continued. "Ben jumped in and out of jobs during the next several years, never trying to succeed at any of them. It was as if he was trying to fail. He rented an art studio away from the house which only added to our debt. He spent most of his time there. I needed to change my life, but didn't know how. But I was at a bookstore one day, when a book by Catherine Ponder fell off the shelf and into my hands. Have you heard of her?"

# CHAPTER THIRTY-THREE

"YES, I'VE READ most of Ponder's books, and have found them inspiring," Jake said.

"Yes, her books are like a breath of fresh air. I read them often. But when I asked Ben to read her books, he wouldn't. So I'd tell him what I was learning, and how we needed to change our mindset to improve our lives. But this made him moodier. He rather enjoyed seeing himself as a victim."

"The brooding artist, eh?" Jake asked.

"Something like that. Then one night, after reading one of Ponder's books, I realized that worrying about money meant I was focusing on lack. If I wanted to change my life, I needed to focus on what I wanted instead. I had to shift my energy. Do you know what I mean?"

Jake nodded and said, "Yes, thought plus emotion equals result. Everything happens in alignment with our deepest and most resilient beliefs."

"I may use that in a workshop."

"Fine by me," he said.

"Thanks. Should I continue?"

"Why stop in the middle of a story?"

"Okay. So I decided to stop worrying and start trusting, like Ponder taught. Worry did no good. Worry was negative prayer. I started telling it like I wanted it to be. I became thankful and grateful for all the good in my life and for what I desircd. And I started asking spirit for help and guidance."

"Maybe that's why you went through all that. It may have been a roundabout way to get there, but in hindsight it served you," Jake said.

"Yes, you may be right. And because of all I went through, I can relate to my client's when they talk about their own dark night of the soul. Whatever the reason, my intuition grew stronger once I made the decision to seek the answers from within and trust my guidance. And in relying on the still small voice within, I felt better about myself.

"I had hoped our marriage would improve, but instead it got worse. Now that I look back, it was like a festering wound coming to a head so healing could take place. But I didn't see it that way at the time. And Ben acted threatened by my inner journey. Why is it that those closest to us can be the least supportive? It's as if they don't want us to change, even when we are in misery."

"It's kind of like crabs," Jake said.

"Crabs? What do you mean?"

Jake smiled and said, "When I was young, my family would drive out to the coast to go crabbing. Dad would toss the crabs we caught into a tub. I'd sit by the tub watching the crabs trying to escape. But not one of them ever made it out because the crabs pulled each other down."

"Yes, some people act threatened when we strive to improve ourselves. They pull us back even if our changing would benefit the clan. And in our clan, the only crab that mattered was Ben, the king crab. Any talk about my dreams, goals and desires annoyed him."

"So when did you figure out he was cheating on you?" Jake asked.

His comment surprised me. "Is it that obvious? I guess there were telltale signs, but I chose to ignore them. His ego needed constant stroking, and someone else was giving it to him."

"She was stroking his ego, or stroking his...?"

I laughed, "Both, I guess. It was too painful to admit Ben was cheating. I wanted to save our marriage, but he was hardly ever home."

Jake said, "And he wouldn't want you to be psychic because he didn't want you to know what he was up to. That's why he never supported your Gifts."

"That never occurred to me," I said with a sigh. "I can't believe how naive I was, but it turns out our breakup was for the best. I would not have become a professional medium had I stayed married to him."

"So you divorced him."

"No, he divorced me."

Jake looked startled, and said, "I expected you to say you had enough and left him."

"No, I kept hoping to salvage our marriage, even when he was cheating."

"So what happened?"

"Ben left me. He said it was because I never supported him. But friends told me Ben's model was living at his studio. He told this friend that his muse had given him an ultimatum... her or me. So that's when he asked me for the divorce. And while it hurt, I also felt relieved."

"And Jasmine was that model?"

I shook my head. "Oh, no, not Jasmine, though she could have been a model. No, the model's name was Renee. But I heard it wasn't long before she realized Ben's star wasn't rising fast enough to please her. After she left him, several other women moved in and out of his studio. A few months after the divorce the same friend told me Ben had chosen celibacy. He wanted to focus all his energy on his art, and his art soared to a new level. That's when he met Jasmine. It's as if he had to rise up to a new level of thought or energy to align with hers."

"So Jasmine had nothing to do with your divorce?"

"No, they didn't meet till after our divorce. And as much as I hate to admit it, she's a great influence on Ben and his work. She has molded him into the successful artist he is today."

Jake sipped his coffee and asked, "Do you feel guilty about it?"

"Are you asking if I think I failed Ben? Or wonder why I couldn't do for him what Jasmine could?"

"Something like that."

"Perhaps a part of me does. But when I look back at it, I realize our divorce ended up being good for both of us. And our union resulted in Kate and Nathan and those beautiful grandchildren."

Jake totaled his imaginary score card, then tore it in half and tossed it into the air. "We needn't worry about repeating what happened between you and Ben. I won't ask you to support my art. As far as I know, my ego's in check. And I promise to never cheat on you."

I leaned in and kissed him. If I had to go through all I had to be blessed with my children and grandchildren, my Sunflowers Shoppe and Jake, the journey had been worth it.

"Well, if you don't mind my asking," he said, "how did you get out of debt? How could you afford to open Sunflowers?"

"My father died many years ago, leaving my mother as his heir. When my mother died two years ago, I was her sole heir, inheriting her house and other investments. I liquidated her assets, and with what I saved from my salary at the firm, I had enough money to pay off all my debts and open my store."

Jake nodded, then stared at the lake, sipping his coffee. What was he thinking about? I felt a tingle of embarrassment at having spoken so long about my life.

As if sensing my unease, Jake said, "You can tell me anything, Jen. I love you and I like getting to know you better. And I enjoy being with you."

A rush of love and relief washed over me. "I feel the same about you."

"I hope you do, because there's something I'd like to ask you."

"Oh? What is it?"

"I'd like to spend more time with you. In fact, I'd like to spend the rest of my life with you," Jake said as he pulled a small jewelry box from the pocket of his jacket. I stared at the box as Jake opened it. "Will you marry me?"

As I gazed at the dazzling diamond engagement ring in the box, it took my breath away. This was so unexpected. Was I ready for this?

"Too soon?" Jake asked at my delay in responding to his question.

Tears of joy swelled in my eyes as I hugged him, my heart pounding.

"Is that a yes?" he asked.

I nodded, as I pulled back and looked at him. "Yes, it is yes," I said.

"I love you, Jennie," Jake said as he slipped the ring on my finger.

"I love you, Jake."

# CHAPTER THIRTY-FOUR

ON FRIDAY WE visited Brasstown Bald. At 4784 feet it is the highest elevation in Georgia. We reached the summit by hiking the steep one-half mile trail that climbed 500 feet in elevation from where we started our trek. And I read that settlers had derived the name *Brasstown* by confusing the Cherokee word for *New Green Place* with the similar sounding one for *Brass*.

The hike was exhilarating, and the views from the observation tower were breathtaking. And the mountaintop visitor center's museum and film was educational. And I enjoyed the views, the history, and the flora. But I must confess that every glance at Jake and at my new engagement ring was the most titillating. I felt giddy about our engagement and the promise of our future together. I was so in love that I wanted to shout it from the mountaintop and let it echo in the valley below. I had never dreamt I would be this happy!

After our hike, we were too tired to walk around the shops in Helen, so instead dined at a lakeside restaurant in Hiawassee.

☼

On Saturday we planned to explore the town of Helen, to tour the shops and have dinner. But first we were invited for brunch next door at Stan and Margot's house. Jake and I walked hand in hand across the connecting yards and up the steps to their porch. Jake knocked on the screen door.

Two little boys ran out, looked at us from behind the screen, then ran back into the house. A man came to the door, opened it and said, "Hi, Jake. It's great to see you."

"Good to see you too, Stan," Jake said as they shook hands. "This is Jennie."

"Hello, Jennie. Nice to meet you," Stan said. "Come in."

We followed him across the porch and into the house, where a woman said, "Hi, Jake."

Jake said, "Hi Margot, this is Jennie."

With the most cordial smile, Margot said, "It's nice to meet you. Welcome to our home."

"Thank you," I said.

Margot and Stan ushered us to the living room. We took a seat on the sofa, and I admired the blazing fireplace and homey cottage. The boys ran into the room and climbed onto Stan's lap.

Stan laughed with delight at their antics and said, "This is Brent and Bobby, our grandsons. We've had the privilege of spending the morning alone with them while their parents are out shopping." He looked at the clock on the mantel and said, "They should be here any minute."

"Hi Brent. Hi Bobby," I said. Bobby looked to be the older of the two, but not by much. "I have a grandson about your age, Brent. His name is Evan."

Brent smiled and leaned back against his grandfather's chest.

"So tell us, Jake, what's new?" Stan said.

Jake smiled and held my hand. "Jennie and I are engaged."

"What? Well isn't that fantastic!" Stan said.

"Oh, that's wonderful," Margot said as she gazed at my ring. "Congratulations!"

"Thank you," Jake said as he hugged me. "I'm one lucky fellow."

"Yes, you are," Stan said with a nod and a smile.

"This calls for celebration," Margot said and dashed to the kitchen. She returned carrying a tray and served us wine and the boys juice. We all stood up, raised our glasses in a toast and Stan said, "We wish you both the greatest happiness for many years to come."

"Thank you," Jake and I said. We all clinked glasses, and reached down to clink the juice glasses the boys held.

Margot hugged Jake, and said, "We are so happy for you and your news."

"Thank you," he said. "You're the first to hear it."

"We're honored," Stan said.

The front door opened, and the boys ran to the young couple entering the house. "Mommy!" yelled Brent. The young woman picked him up as Bobby hugged her leg.

"What about Daddy?" the man said.

"Hi, Daddy," Brent said from his mother's arms. Bobby walked over to the man and hugged him.

When his mother set Brent on the floor he tugged her hand toward us. "Just a minute, Brent," she said. "Daddy and I have to take off our coats."

"He's quite a mama's boy," Margot said. "I wish he was closer to Darryl."

I watched Brent hovering near his mother, and said, "That's not unusual for his age."

Margot shrugged.

"Darryl is Margot's boy," Stan said with a nod toward the boy's father. "She worries over our son constantly."

"That's not true," Margot said in a loud whisper. "I just wish both boys were more bonded with him."

"What are you talking about?" Darryl asked as he joined us in the living room.

"Oh, it's nothing," Stan said with a wave of dismissal. "Hey, you remember Jake, don't you Darryl?"

Darryl's face lit in recognition. "Jake! It's been a while. How are you?" he asked as they shook hands.

"I'm great, thanks for asking," Jake said, then turned toward me and said. "And I'd like you to meet my fiancée, Jennie."

"Your fiancée? Congratulations to you both! It's nice to meet you, Jennie."

"What's this? Is there news?" his wife asked as she joined us.

"Yes," Darryl said. "Meet Jake's fiancée."

"Your fiancée?"

"Yes, Rita," Jake said, "this is Jennie."

Rita hugged me. "Congratulations."

"Thank you," I said.

"When did you get engaged?" Darryl asked.

"Two days ago," Jake said.

"Wow, no kidding!"

"No kidding," Jake said. He leaned toward me and whispered, "I like saying you're my fiancée."

"So I noticed," I said and smiled. "I like the sound of it, too."

Margot said, "Well, let's eat." We followed her into the dining room. Margot and Stan sat at the opposite ends of the table. Jake and I sat with Bobby across from Darryl, Rita and Brent.

Each place setting included a glass of sweet tea. And in the center of the table was a platter of sliced ham, a basket of rolls and bowls of sweet potatoes and peas.

As we served the food, Rita asked, "Do you have children, Jennie?"

"Yes, I have a son and a daughter. They are each married and I have three grandchildren."

"Grandchildren, huh? What will they call you, Jake?" Darryl said.

Jake looked at me and shrugged. "I hadn't thought about it. I guess they'll call me Jake."

"Oh, that won't do," I said. "It'll be interesting to see what name they come up with."

"It's up to them to name me?" Jake asked.

I nodded. "My children called my parents Opa and Oma."

"Who named you Nana?" Jake asked.

"I asked them to use that in honor of both my grandmothers."

Stan smiled. "Bobby christened us Granddad and Gammaw, and it stuck."

"Yes, and the boys have three sets of grandparents," Darryl said.

"Three?" I said.

"Yes," Rita said, "Stan and Margot, my parents and their birth father's parents."

I had assumed Darryl was their birth father. Now I understood Margot's concern about them bonding with her son.

Rita patted her belly, and said, "But this baby will only have two sets of grandparents."

Stan and Margot looked surprised. Margot said, "You're pregnant?"

Rita and Darryl both nodded.

"They're having twins," Mica said at my ear.

"Oh, my God, so much to celebrate today," Margot said. "I'm overjoyed!"

We all raised our sweet tea glasses and toasted the happy couple. But I sensed they had not always been so happy. '*What was I sensing?*' I silently asked my guide.

"Conflict," Mica said. "Rita didn't want Darryl to discipline her sons. But she has realized he is a great father. Bobby and Brent are bonding with Darryl now that they sense their mother trusting him."

I nodded at Mica's information.

"What's up?" Jake asked.

"Oh," I said and blushed as I realized I had nodded, "everything's just so delicious."

"Yes, everything is," Jake said with a look that told me he suspected there was more to my nod, but we'd talk later.

"I'm glad you like it," Margot said.

☼

After lunch, I helped Margot clear the table. As she washed and rinsed the dishes, I dried them. She handed me a plate and said, "I hope the new baby is closer to my son."

"I'm sure they will be," I said.

"They?" she said.

Oops, '*Was she open to my being a medium?*'

"Tread lightly," Mica said.

"I mean he or she," I said, "Darryl's child will likely have an instant bond to his, or her father."

"But that's what I don't understand," Margot said. "Darryl has been the only father the boys have known. They never knew their birth father. Bobby's doing better, but Brent still clings to his mother."

"Everything will work out fine, and Brent will bond more with Darryl after the birth of the baby."

"How can you be so sure?"

I shrugged. "Just a hunch," I said.

# CHAPTER THIRTY-FIVE

IT WAS HARD to leave the lake house Sunday morning, but it was easier knowing we'd return in a few months. And Jake suggested we invite the whole family here in the summer. So I looked forward to having everyone together, enjoying the lake.

The ride along I-75 had been uneventful. When we were south of the city of Atlanta, Jake said, "Do you like fried chicken?"

"On occasion," I said, "but only if it's not greasy."

"Then you are in for a treat," he said as he exited the highway. We drove down a two-lane country road, and as we rounded a bend Jake pulled into the parking lot of the Buckner's Family Style Restaurant.

"This is my favorite stop on the trip. The food is fast and delicious."

We entered the lobby and Jake paid for our dinners. We followed the hostess to a large round table, where she seated us with six other people who had also just entered the restaurant. At first it was awkward to sit for a meal with total strangers. But I looked around the room and saw tables of fellow travelers enjoying their food.

A waitress pushed a cart laden with platters and bowls of food to our table. The food smelled and looked delicious as she placed the entire buffet in the center. There were platters of fried chicken, roast beef, and green beans. Stewed tomatoes, mashed potatoes, creamed corn, beans, and coleslaw. Corn bread, cobbler, and condiments all rotating and within easy reach on the lazy susan.

"Eat all you want," Jake said with a grin, "they'll bring more."

"What'll you have to drink?" the waitress asked.

"Sweet tea," Jake said.

I nodded. "I'll have sweet tea, too."

We piled our plates with food, and I said, "Is this what they call family style?"

"I guess so," Jake said. "There's no menu. You just sit down and eat what the cook made."

The food was delicious! "How did you find this place?"

"My folks found out about it years ago, and it became a family tradition to stop in whenever we were in the area. Only problem is, they're not open every day."

"Well, it was a good find," I said, and sat back patting my belly. "It's so good."

"Yes, but it's so delicious you can't stop eating."

I glanced at my watch, "Guess we won't need dinner."

☼

As we neared the Florida border, I basked in the afterglow of our weekend together. Every moment, every meal, the hiking, the boat ride, the love making and the ring; especially the ring.

But I couldn't shake an uneasiness from last night's dream. I felt dread, that something awful was going to happen. I told Jake about it, and said, "Kate doesn't want me to intrude in her privacy, but what if this dream is a warning? What if I don't say anything and something happens that I could have prevented? I can't shake this foreboding."

"Instead of calling Kate, why not call Brad?"

"That's a good idea," I said and called his cell phone.

He answered on the second ring. "Hi, Nana," he said, "what's up?"

"Jake and I are driving home from Georgia, and I'd like to tell you about my dream."

"Why me?"

"When I tell it to you, you'll understand."

"Okay, shoot."

"Last night, I dreamt that Evan's headboard came off his bed. I'm concerned he'll get hurt. Will you check it? Maybe it's damaged or missing a screw or something."

Brad chuckled, and said, "We replaced his headboard over the weekend. You must have picked up on that, or the need to replace it."

"That must be it," I said, feeling somewhat relieved. "You know how Kate feels about my intruding, so that's why I phoned you. I was worried Evan was in danger."

"Hey, I'd rather you warn us, even if it turns out to be nothing. So how was your trip?"

"It was wonderful," I said admiring my ring. "We'll have to get with you and Kate to tell you all about it."

"When will you be home?" he said.

"Later tonight."

"Okay. Well, drive safe, and we'll see you soon."

"Thanks, Brad, and thank you for being so understanding."

"No worries, Nana. Call me anytime."

I disconnected and told Jake about the headboard. "It's odd, though," I said. "I thought that was it, but I still have foreboding."

"Maybe it's a residue from the dream?"

"Could be," I said, "I hope so."

Jake parked the Jeep in front of Sunflowers, and turned off the ignition. "Back to reality," he said.

"I miss the lake, but Sunflowers is a pleasing sight," I said.

I opened the store's front door, and Jake helped carry my things inside. As much as I enjoyed our trip, it felt good to be home. I walked ahead of him, switching on the hall light. We stopped at my apartment door as I unlocked it, and brought my suitcase and packages into the room. "Do you want anything to eat?" I said.

"No, I'm full and tired," he said.

"Do you want to sleep here tonight?"

"Yeah, I'll go get my overnight bag. But we have to talk about this soon."

"About what?"

"Where we'll live," he said, and walked back to the Jeep.

Where will we live? Will I give up my apartment? Will Jake move in here? Will I move to his house? Will we get a new house?

I was too tired to think about it tonight, and got ready for bed. After not sleeping well last night, I was in need of a good night's sleep. And I hoped that come morning the foreboding would be gone.

By the time Jake came to bed, I was under the covers and fast asleep.

# CHAPTER THIRTY-SIX

THE SOUND OF my cell phone ringing woke me. I glanced at the clock, it was just past midnight. I'd only slept a few hours. I picked up the phone and looked at the caller ID. It was my daughter's number. I answered in a whisper so as not to disturb Jake.

"Kate? What is it?"

Kate was crying. "Mom, I need you!"

"What is it, what's wrong?"

"I need you to come here. It's... it's..."

An entity appeared by the foot of my bed. "Brad?" I said, stunned. Why was I seeing him?

"Yes, it's Brad," she said. "Please come. I need you!"

"What's wrong? What happened?" I asked as I stared at the vision of my son-in-law.

"Brad was in an accident. He drove into a tree. I guess he swerved to avoid hitting someone who had pulled out in front of him."

"Oh my God!" I said sitting up in bed, now fully awake. "Are you okay? How are the children?"

"We weren't in the car. Please come!"

"I'm on my way." I said, and disconnected the call.

"Who was that?" Jake asked, groggy with sleep.

"It was Kate," I said. Brad's spirit still stood at the foot of the bed. "Why are you here?" I asked.

"Why is who here? Who are you talking to?" Jake asked as he followed my gaze.

"Brad. He's right there," I said, and pointed at the vision. "Why are you here?" I looked at Jake, and said, "He's confused."

"So am I," Jake said.

Brad disappeared, and I got out of bed and ran to the bathroom.

"Where are you going?" Jake asked as he followed me.

"I'm going to Kate. She needs me," I said as I quickly dressed and grabbed my purse.

"I'll drive you," Jake said as he pulled on his clothes.

"But I don't know how long I'll be with her."

"That's okay. I'll drive you there now, and I'll come back for you when you're ready to come home."

"That's too much to ask. I'll just go."

"No! You are too upset to drive."

"Jake, please, I don't have time to argue. I have to go to Kate," I said, and grabbed my still packed suitcase off the floor.

Jake took the suitcase from my hand as we raced down the hall and out the front door. Jake waited while I locked the store, then placed my suitcase in his Jeep.

I felt numb, nauseous, and frantic all at the same time as the feeling of foreboding returned. *'Was Brad okay?'* I asked my guide.

"You need to be strong for Kate," Mica said. "And Brad doesn't realize he's dead. Tell him to go to the light."

I burst into tears. No, It can't be! I can't bear it!

"What's wrong?" Jake asked.

"Brad's dead!"

"How do you know? Did Kate tell you that?"

"No, Mica just did. Why didn't I see this coming? Why didn't I receive a warning, a dream, or a message? What good are my Gifts if I can't help my family?"

Jake shook his head, looking puzzled as he drove as fast as he could to Kate's house.

When we arrived, Jake parked in Kate's driveway, and followed me as I ran to the front door. I was about to knock when the door opened. A woman, who looked to be about Kate's age, stood in the doorway. "You must be Kate's mother," she said.

"Yes, I am," I said.

"I'm Shelly, Kate's neighbor. Please come in."

"Where's Kate?" I asked as we stepped into the foyer.

"She's in her bedroom. She's expecting you. I came over when she called me. I didn't want her to be alone. Evan and Lola are sleeping. We didn't wake them, so she hasn't told them, yet." Shelly started toward the front door, then stopped. "My phone number is on a notepad on the fridge. Call me if you need anything," she said.

"Thank you," I said.

Jake locked the door behind her, and said, "Go on in to Kate. I'll wait in the living room."

I opened Kate's bedroom door and stepped into her room. She was on her bed, swaddled in a quilt and surrounded by wads of tissue. Was she asleep? No, her shoulders were shaking, she was sobbing. I set my purse on her dresser and walked up to her bed. "Kate?"

Kate looked up at me. "Oh, Mommy!"

She reached for me and I sat down and hugged her. I rocked her and cooed to her like when she was a child. "I'm here, Kate. Mommy's here," I said. She sobbed as I comforted her, holding back my own tears as I allowed hers.

She pulled away, blew her nose, and looked at me. Even in the darkened room, she looked very pale.

"Oh, Mommy, how can Brad be gone? How?"

"Tell me what happened."

"We were about to get ready for bed, when he opened the refrigerator for a bottled water. I was already in the bedroom, when he came in the room and said we were out of milk. I told him it could wait till tomorrow. He said the kids would need it for their breakfast. I said they could have eggs instead of cereal. But he insisted, and said he'd be right back. And now he's gone. And it's all my fault!"

"How is it your fault?"

"Because if I hadn't forgotten to buy milk, he wouldn't have gone out for it." Kate blew her nose and tossed the wadded tissue, missing the basket on the floor. "After he left, I went to bed and fell asleep. The police woke me and told me about Brad. I called Shelly and asked her to wait with me till you got here."

"That's good, you shouldn't be alone now."

She cried and said, "Oh, Mom, what am I going to do without Brad?"

As she sobbed, I wondered the same thing. She and Brad had been inseparable since the day they met. They were so in love, so happy, and had their whole lives ahead of them.

"Will you help me make the arrangements," she said.

"Of course."

"His parents are trying to book a flight here today. That's the hardest call I've ever made," she said, and sobbed.

"Yes, I'm sure it was."

"We need to have his service tomorrow or the next day."

"Whatever has to get done, we'll do," I said.

"Brad and I never talked about death. It was too morbid, and we never dreamt it would happen to either of us so soon. But the one discussion we had, he said he'd want to be cremated." She sobbed again, then said, "But I don't know if I can do that to him."

"It just speeds up the process, Honey; but you do what you need to do."

"Do you think Lola and Evan should see him? Should they go to the funeral?"

I shuddered. "That's up to you. We'll do what you need to do."

# CHAPTER THIRTY-SEVEN

## *Wednesday*

I SAT THROUGH Brad's funeral for my daughter's sake. Shelly had been kind enough to take the children for the day and overnight. Her children were a welcomed distraction for them. It had been difficult telling Evan and Lola about their father, and Kate and I were trying to be conscious of their needs and concerns.

Nathan had flown down from Ohio. Kate sat between us in the pew. Jake sat in the row behind me, being strong for me so I could be strong for my daughter. The packed funeral home showed that in his too short life, Brad was well liked and loved. He had been a good man, friend, husband, father and son.

It was then I realized that people grieve in different ways. While I saw Brad as still alive in spirit, others viewed his body as the man they loved. What to me was an empty vessel that once held his very alive spirit, they saw as the person, the personality, they still cherished.

From my seat I could see the collage of photos Kate had glued to a poster board and placed on an easel at the front of the room. There were photos of Brad as a young boy, as a teenager and when he dated Kate. There was wedding photos, travel photos and photos of Brad with their children.

As I looked at the photographs, I was aware of Brad's spirit walking around the room. He stood by his coffin, then by his parents, then by Kate, then by his friends, and now by me. He knew I saw him. He wanted me to talk to him, but I couldn't, not here, not now.

So I silently communicated to him, *'You have passed on, Brad. There was a car accident. You need to go to the light.'*

He looked startled, and backed away from me with alarm and confusion on his face. I prayed for help. At the far corner of the room a spirit came forth and called to Brad, but he moved closer to Kate.

"He will go with them after the service," Mica said. "He will be okay. He is not alone, and neither are you."

I offered a silent thanks to Mica, and to Brad's guides.

The minister entered the room. He gave his condolences to Kate and to Brad's parents, then stood at the podium acknowledging the mourners. I found his sermon helpful and interesting. He used phrases like, "When a loved one dies we face our own mortality" and "The soul of our loved one lives on".

Kate sobbed, her head on my shoulder while she held Nathan's hand. Ben and Jasmine sat on the other side of Nathan. I was grateful Kate was not alone, but surrounded by those who loved her and Brad.

Finally, the funeral was over. As the mourners exited the room, most stopped to speak with Kate. Brad's employer assured her that the company would help in any way they could. He handed her an envelope and said it contained a donation from Brad's fellow employees.

After the guests left, Kate walked up to the coffin for one last look at her husband, then turned to me and said, "Let's go home."

Nathan and Jake carried an assortment of flowers and the photo board as we left the funeral home. We all piled into Kate's car, and Nathan drove us to her house.

☼

When we walked into the house, Jake pulled me aside and asked, "Do you need anything?"

"Yes, I need a hug."

He hugged me tight, and said, "I'll be in the living room if you need me."

I followed Kate and Nathan into the kitchen, and made each a cup of hot tea.

As I placed the mugs on the table, Kate said, "Is Brad okay?"

I wasn't sure how to respond. "What do you mean?"

"You know... is his soul okay?"

That she asked me a spiritual question surprised me, since she had always refused to discuss the topic. I answered, somewhat tentatively, "It is my belief that the soul, the spirit that was Brad, is eternal. Brad's spirit was not harmed by his physical death, but lives on."

"You really think so?" she asked.

"Yes."

"Do you know so?"

I shrugged. "I believe it's true." I poured a cup of tea for myself, and joined them at the table.

Kate said, "Did you have a premonition this was going to happen?"

"No," I said, feeling uneasy as I shifted in my chair. Why had I not known? I recalled seeing Brad's spirit at the foot of my bed when Kate had first phoned me. The foreboding that had lingered from the dream about Evan's headboard must have had something to do with Brad. But for some reason, it was either not revealed to me during that dream, or I had not recalled it upon awakening.

"What are you frowning about?" Kate asked.

"Oh, it's nothing," I said.

Kate reached across the table, and squeezed my hand. "No, Mom, what is it?"

I told her and Nathan about the dream I had about Evan's bed. I told them I had phoned Brad about it, and said, "That's all I remembered about the dream. If Brad was in it, I don't recall it, even now."

"If I hadn't banned your abilities from my life, you could have warned us. It's all my fault!" she said, and sobbed.

Nathan jumped from his seat, and hugged his sister. "Don't say that, Kate. It's no one's fault," he said.

"It is my fault. I'm the one who forgot to buy the milk. And I'm the one who shut Mom out."

"Nathan is right, this is no one's fault," I said. "Stop talking like that, don't even think it. You didn't cause this, and you couldn't have stopped it from happening."

"Maybe not, but you could have," she said.

Nathan paced the floor while I pondered her accusation.

"That's not for certain, Kate. If I had seen it coming, it might not have made any difference," I said.

She wept cradling her head with her hands, a captive of her own hellish thoughts and emotions.

"Listen to me, Kate," I said.

She looked up at me.

"Our life is an experience for our soul. It's possible that the time of our passing is as predetermined as the time of our birth. And even if I had been forewarned, would it have made a difference? Brad might have shrugged off the warning, and went to the store anyway. Or he might have had a different accident, or passed another way. But his passing is not your fault, not my fault, and not Brad's fault. It just is what it is."

Kate wiped her tears. "You really think so?"

"Yes."

"I agree with Mom," Nathan said as he took his seat. "You've got to stop beating yourself up over this. It's not going to do you any good, and you have to think about your kids."

"That's right," I said, "you need to be strong for your children. They need you."

"But how can I go on without Brad?"

Her words frightened me. She must realize how vital she is to her children, and to us. "It's going to take time, but you will be okay. Some days will be harder than others, but you'll be okay. You might take two steps forward and one step back, but you will be okay," I said as I tried to convince her... and me... this was true.

We sipped our tea, then Nathan said, "I forgot Jake was in the living room. Maybe he wants some tea."

"I'll go ask him," I said. I walked into the living room and found Jake sitting on the sofa reading a golf magazine. "You want a cup of tea?"

"I'm okay. But I'm here if you need me."

"Why don't you join us?"

"You sure?"

"Yes, you're going to be part of the family."

"He is?" Kate asked as she walked into the room carrying her tea and handing a second cup to Jake.

"Yes, he is," I said as I sat next to Jake. "I was going to tell you our news, but was waiting for the right time."

"Right time for what?" Nathan asked as he followed Kate into the room and handed me my cup of tea. "Did I miss something?"

Kate noticed the ring on my finger, and said, "You're engaged?" I nodded as she took my hand for a closer look at the ring. "I'm sorry I hadn't noticed. But it's wonderful news, and I'm happy for both of you!"

Nathan studied Jake a moment. "Does Jake make you happy, Mom?"

"Yes," I said, "he does."

"Congratulations then," Nathan said, and shook Jake's hand. We all stood up, and I hugged Kate, then Nathan. As Kate hugged Jake, Nathan said, "Welcome to the family."

"Thank you," Jake said.

We took our seats, and Kate said, "Okay, Mom, tell me about your store, your Gifts, what you do, and why you do it. Tell me everything!"

This was so unexpected, I wasn't sure where to begin. But once we started talking about the store, mediumship and spirituality, we couldn't stop, and talked into the wee hours of the morning.

# CHAPTER THIRTY-EIGHT

I TOLD KATE, Nathan and Jake that I could hear and see spirits since I was a child. But my friends mocked my sensitivities, and my mother discouraged my abilities. So I tucked away my Gifts from fear of being different.

"I'd have a premonition, dream messages or forebodings," I said, "but it was random. In time I learned that the more I paid attention, the more my Gifts opened up. I sought to hone my skills to better rely on them. So I read a lot of books and attended classes. I learned that we, our spirit, is alive after so called death. I now view the afterlife as more real than this one. Death is simply our spirit passing to another frequency, and going home.

"When he arrives home, on the other side, the spirit remembers who he really is... a spiritual being who had an Earthly experience. And since most of our spirit doesn't enter the Earth body, that larger part of us, what we call our higher self, welcomes the soul home. Once reunited in spirit, amnesia falls away and knowledge returns. The soul can recall his most recent life, along with every incarnation. Not just while on Earth, but in other planes and dimensions as well. And the being aligns and resonates fully again with the greatest power there is... Divine Love.

"At some point, the spirit is counseled during his life review. But he is his own judge and jury and decides the next path of his spiritual journey. Our spirit chooses whether, when and where to incarnate. And it is during this review that the spirit realizes if he wronged someone or hindered their progress. If so, the spirit might try to communicate with that person directly, or in dreams, or through a medium. Not all psychics are mediums, but all mediums are psychic. Psychics read energy while mediums communicate with spirits, acting as a transceiver.

"The medium interprets for the spirit communicator to the recipient, known as the sitter during a reading. Evidential mediums deliver evidence using one or more of the paranormal senses. These include clairaugustance, which is psychically tasting or smelling something. Clairvoyance, as in psychic seeing, clairaudience is hearing. Clairsencience is feeling, and clairomniscience is a knowing, when receiving a flash of inspired thought. This evidence can include a description of the spirit, or a mannerism, or an event, or the personality as known to the sitter.

"Once the evidence is delivered, the medium gives the spirit's message. The message often helps the sitter release resentment, anger, guilt, fear, or worry. The message often has universal meaning which can also benefit others. But sometimes the spirit simply wants to connect, to be remembered, or to tell a loved one he is okay. At times, the spirit can be humorous. But the spirits are always wise and loving, which I believe is our natural state of being."

Kate, Nathan and Jake hadn't commented while I spoke, but when I finished Kate said, "Wow, I had no idea!"

Nathan said, "Your work is so important!"

And Jake said, "Your mother is very good at what she does. You should be proud of her. I am."

"Thank you, but I don't see it as my being special. The work is not about me. I am an instrument assisting the spirit world."

"That may be, but I'm still proud of you. And you may have just given us your first workshop," Jake said.

I smiled, and nodded in agreement.

"Where do you think the afterlife is?" Nathan asked.

"I tend to believe it's here, in a higher dimension or vibration, and it's accessed by a virtual doorway, on the other side of the veil. And I've read that what we first experience after our passing aligns with our beliefs; and we meet who we expect. And it's possible we glimpse, or visit the astral realms during sleep. And isn't it interesting how some dreams seem so real? I've awakened feeling as if I've taken a journey, attended a lecture, or met with someone I know or knew. Some nights seem especially busy, as if I was doing a task or solving a problem all night long. But most of my dreams contain a symbolic or prophetic message or remnant," I said.

"So where is Brad now? And what is he doing?" Kate asked.

"He is with his spiritual family, guides and teachers. His spirit being is doing whatever it is we do on that side of the veil, while we tend to life on this side of it. Be comforted, Kate. Brad is not alone, but neither are you. We are all helped by our guides, and guided by our higher self."

"It sometimes feels like Brad is near me. Is that possible?" Kate said.

"Yes, of course," I said.

"Will I dream about being with him?" Kate asked.

"Yes, I'm certain you will, and may already have. Brad's love for you transcends space and time. Fear not, he still loves you, and he will always remember you."

# CHAPTER THIRTY-NINE

DURING BREAKFAST THE following morning, I told Nathan and Kate that Jake and I had planned to travel to Ohio for Christmas. "But I don't want to leave Kate and the children alone now during the holidays," I said. "I hope you understand, Nathan."

Nathan said, "Actually, Bridgette and I discussed it on the phone last night and have decided to come here for Christmas, too. We don't want Kate to be alone either, and I think Emily would enjoy being with Lola and Evan."

Kate was quite pleased and grateful that she and her children would be surrounded by family for the holidays. We all agreed that it was the thing to do. "Brad's parents said they'd like to be here for Christmas, too," Kate said. "I told them they were welcome to join us. With Dad and Jasmine coming over Christmas Day too, it's gonna be a full house!"

As we finished eating breakfast, Shelly phoned Kate to say she'd take Lola and Evan to daycare. I had hoped they'd come home, but Kate said daycare was a good idea as she needed to rest.

Nathan set his suitcase by the front door, ready to leave for his flight to Ohio, eager to get home to his wife and daughter. Jake had offered to drive him to the airport on his way home to Del Vista. He was due back to work at the pro shop tomorrow morning. I wanted to stay with Kate for a few more days, before going back to Sunflowers and life as usual.

We said our tearful goodbyes, then watched as Jake and Nathan drove away. I already missed them, but I would be with Jake soon. And being that Nathan would be back at Christmas made his goodbye less painful.

The house was quiet with Kate and I alone. Her life without her husband / best friend started today. Kate hugged me, then went to her bedroom and shut the door. Unsure whether to hover or give her space, I looked at her closed door and decided to meditate.

Coming out of meditation, I decided it was best to act as 'normal' as possible. I'd do the laundry, straighten the house and cook dinner. Those kinds of routine activities might help us both get more grounded.

I started in the children's rooms, where I made their beds and put away their toys. In their bathroom I tossed all the towels and washcloths into the clothes hamper, and carried it to the utility room. I started a load in the washing machine, then cleared the breakfast dishes from the table and loaded the dishwasher.

When I finished cleaning the kitchen, I planned to vacuum, but decided to not disturb Kate's rest. I debated whether to check in on her, then knocked lightly on her door. She didn't answer. Had I been foolish to leave her alone? Was she suicidal?

Alarmed, I opened the door and found her laying on the bed. I walked up to her, relieved to find no empty pill bottles on her mattress or nightstand. I leaned toward her for a closer look.

She opened her eyes, startled to see me, and startling me. "What is it?" she asked.

"Just checking on you," I said.

"I need to sleep. I haven't gotten much lately."

"I was going to vacuum, but didn't want to disturb you."

"Can it wait?"

"Of course."

"We'll do it later, Mom. I need to rest." I kissed her forehead, and turned to leave the room, when she said, "Will you lay down with me?"

I walked over to the other side of her bed, kicked off my shoes and laid down. I wasn't sleepy, but as soon as I closed my eyes, I was dreaming. I dreamt of Brad's collision, and saw the tree coming at the windshield. I felt his panic at realizing the tree was unavoidable. I viewed his spirit releasing from his body before impact and the airbag exploding.

I caught glimpses of what Brad had seen of the emergency workers, the hospital, and the funeral home. And I saw the spiritual being who had come forward to escort him into the light. This being had been one of his grandparents. The dream ended, and I opened my eyes.

*'Do I tell Kate about the dream? Do I give her a reading?'*

"No," Mica said. "When the time comes, let her first reading be with Sara."

Yes, my instructor would be better as she'd be emotionally detached. I could offer to sit with Kate for moral support, but I won't push her.

"She'll ask for one when she's ready, if she ever chooses to have one," Mica said.

While Kate slept, I recalled images of her as an infant, as a toddler, as my sweet little girl. I wished I could have protected her from this traumatic event. But life held many mysteries about why we experience what we do. Brad had blessed Kate's life with Evan and Lola, and in numerous other ways. He had been a wonderful husband to my girl. I hoped that someday, while never looking to replace him, she will find another loving relationship.

Kate tossed and murmured something, then laughed in her sleep. What had she dreamt that could be so humorous? Not wanting to wake her, I stared at the ceiling as she slept. Fifteen minutes later Kate opened her eyes.

"How are you doing?" I asked.

She rubbed her eyes as she sat up, and said, "I guess I got some sleep."

"Yes, you did. And you laughed in your sleep. Do you remember that?"

"I did? I don't remember it."

"Lay on the pillow and close your eyes. Invite the dream to come back to you. Just allow it without reaching for it."

She closed her eyes a minute, then opened them and said, "I dreamt I was talking with Brad. He said that when we first met he felt shy in approaching me. I found that funny." Kate sat up and said, "It felt like I was with him. It was more than thinking about him, it was as if I visited with him. You know what I mean?"

"Yes, I do. It's a more lucid dream."

"Yes, I guess so."

"I had a dream something like that after your grandmother died. My mother and I loved to shop and have lunch together. A few weeks after she passed away, I dreamt I was riding with her in a car. We chatted like old times as she drove. When I awoke, it had been more than a dream, I had been with her."

"Yes, that's what I mean!"

"Those dreams are precious gifts and make me wonder, which is the real world and which is the world of dreams?"

"Yes, it does make you think. It felt so good to have Brad near me. I hope I dream that way of him again," Kate said and stood from the bed and stretched. "I think I'll take a long shower."

I got off the bed and asked, "Do you want me to toss your sheets in the washer?"

She shook her head as she looked at them. "No, not yet, I don't want to wash away Brad's scent. I may never wash his pillow case," she said as she hugged his pillow to her and took in a deep breath. It was the pillow she had been sleeping on.

"No need to ever wash that pillow case, if it comforts you."

"Yes, I may never wash it," she said, hugged the pillow again and placed it on the bed. She walked toward her bathroom as I left the room.

In the utility room I tossed a load of towels from the washer into the dryer. I started another load, then pulled the vacuum to the living room. Years ago when my mother needed to ponder something, she'd iron. Nowadays, there was not much ironing to do, but one can always vacuum.

The vacuum roared to life when I flipped the switch. From the monotony of the chore, my mind drifted back to when Kate was young, sleeping with her security blanket. Now she sought that comfort with Brad's pillow.

After Kate's shower, we picked the children up early from daycare. They filled the house with their activity and vitality.

Kate spent quality time alone with each child, and we all took a long nap together. Afterwards we played games until dinnertime, and read stories before they went to bed.

# CHAPTER FORTY

THE NEXT MORNING, I passed Evan's room and noticed him sitting on his bed. Lola stood next to him, and they were whispering.

"What's up?" I asked as I entered his room.

"Oh, nothing," Lola said, and walked away from her brother, twirling her long hair around her finger.

Evan looked at me with sad eyes. I sat on his bed, and pulled him onto my lap, hugging him. "What were you two talking about?" I asked.

"Did I do something wrong, Nana?" he said.

"What do you mean?"

"Did I make Daddy go away?"

I hugged him again and said, "You did nothing wrong, Evan." I looked at Lola, who was frowning. "And neither did you, Lola. Your daddy loves and watches over both of you."

"I told you, Evan," Lola said.

Evan hugged into me.

"What did you tell him, Lola?" Lola stood in the center of the room, still twisting a long strand of her golden hair with her fingers as she swayed back and forth. "What is it?" I asked.

"Lola saw Daddy," Evan said.

"I told you not to tell!" Lola said.

Evan flinched.

"It's okay, Evan," I said. "When did you see your daddy, Lola?"

"Last night," she said. "He was standing by my bed."

"Did you see him, too, Evan?" I asked.

"No," he said with a whimper.

"And this morning," Lola said as she pointed, "Daddy was standing there, by Evan's bed and looking at him."

Tears welled up in Evan's eyes. "Why didn't I see Daddy?"

"You were sleeping," Lola said.

"What Lola saw was your daddy's spirit," I said. "He was coming to say hi to you. There's nothing to fear."

"I'm not scared of Daddy," Lola said. "But I don't want to tell Mommy."

"Why not?" I asked.

"I don't want to make her cry," she said.

Evan shook his head and said, "I don't want Mommy to cry either."

I motioned for Lola to come to me. I hugged my grandchildren to me. How would Kate handle hearing that Lola has visions? "I can help you," I said. Both children looked up at me. "I'll tell Mommy for you."

"You will?" Lola said.

"Yes, I will," I said.

Lola smiled at me and Evan.

"But I want to see Daddy, too," Evan said.

"Well, even if you don't, know that he is with you and loves you very much," I said.

Evan nodded, and I hugged both children again.

"Thanks, Nana," Lola said. "Come on, Evan, let's go play in my room," she said as she took his hand and pulled him from my lap.

Now how do I tell Kate?

I was sitting at the kitchen table, mindlessly flipping the pages of a magazine, when Kate joined me.

"How are you doing?" she asked.

"I'm doing okay. How about you?"

She shrugged, and said, "I'm taking it moment by moment, and I'm glad the children are playing."

"Yes, me, too," I said as I closed the magazine and set it aside. "And I have something to tell you."

"What is it?"

I told Kate about Lola's visions, and said, "It wasn't scary, it gave her comfort."

Kate nodded, and said, "She must have your Gift."

"It's possible," I said. "Time will tell."

"I wanted to ask you something. Do I have to become a medium to get my own guidance?"

*'Why was her question so loaded with anxiety?'* I asked, and I received my answer. She was accustomed to bouncing ideas off Brad. Now she was winging it alone.

"No, Kate, you don't have to be a medium. Everyone has the spiritual connection. And the more we acknowledge it, the stronger our intuition becomes. Ideally, we shouldn't need anyone else for our answers. But sometimes it's difficult when the question is emotionally charged. But to answer your question, yes, anyone can access guidance from their higher self. We just have to ask."

"How do I do that?" Kate said.

"I've learned that in asking, the answer is the first thought or impression that comes. For example, say one asked, 'Is taking this job aligned with my highest good?'. The answer would be an immediate thought, audible, or knowing. Sometimes we dismiss it because it seems too easy."

"But what if I don't get it that way? Or what if I'm unsure?"

"First do this. Ask your question, then say out loud your response. This is especially helpful with simple yes or no answers. Or try it this way, 'Is taking this job aligned with my highest good?' then say, 'I don't know' to help trigger an answer."

"What if I don't even know what to ask?"

"Then ask for clarity. For example, 'What career is aligned with my highest good?' or 'Which (fill in the blank) serves my soul's purpose best?'. And it's best not to start the question with the word *should*. That word can cause inner conflict and mixed messages. Also, try doing this by writing or typing out the question. Try it using or omitting the line, 'I don't know'. And immediately write the answer. Try variations, like speaking the question as you write. Don't judge what you get or withhold it or debate it; just write it. And I find that when I'm asking with writing, I'll get more of an answer than I do verbally. Experiment and find what works best for you."

"What if I don't get an answer?"

"You will get an answer, so did you negate it? Or your answer may be delayed, so let go and trust it's coming. You may get your answer on a billboard or on television or in a magazine. You might hear it in a song or in conversation. You might suddenly know it while walking, or in the shower, or during a dream. Just trust that you will get your answer. It is coming to you. Believe it because everything is created and realized according to our beliefs. And it's like exercising a muscle, the more we trust the process the stronger the guidance becomes."

"How do I learn to trust it?"

"Intend to," I said. "Start with simpler questions. And sometimes a book, video, or talk will help deepen our belief. For example, I read something written by Myrtle Fillmore, the founder of Unity Church. She wrote that her great faith in God revealed Him to her in her every need. Reading about her strong faith helped reinforce mine. And attending Sara's classes helped me. When I initially enrolled it was not to be a medium, but to find that connection with spirit like I had as a child."

"Thanks, Mom. I'm going to write some questions and see if I get answers," Kate said, and walked from the room.

*'Was my living an hour away from Kate too far to give her emotional support?'*

"No, she'll be okay," Mica said. "She has her job, her friends and neighbors. The children have their daycare, friends, and routine. This will help them heal. They have their life to live and you have yours."

"Thanks, Mica". I am happy to be here for Kate and the children, but I do realize I have to get back to Sunflowers and Jake.

And speaking of Jake, where will we live? His house in Del Vista, or would it be better to start out fresh in a new place? His home wasn't too far a drive from Sunflowers. But I wasn't ready to move in with him yet. And when I do, I can either sublet my apartment or make it an extension of my store. But those decisions can wait for now. My daughter and grandchildren needed my attention today.

# CHAPTER FORTY-ONE

## *December*

IT HAD BEEN three weeks since Brad's funeral, and periodic waves of sadness still came over me when I thought of him. As for Kate, she and the children were taking it one day at a time as they adjusted to life without him. And while I was grateful that my daughter was now asking questions and reading books about spirituality, I was sorry for what had triggered our communication about my passion and career. Staring mortality in the face was often the reason people get curious and interested in the subject.

As for me, Megan was after me to create a workshop for January. With the new year approaching, she had been busy creating posters, fliers, and updating our new website. But when she told me that Kate had submitted our online workshop attendance form, I got busy too! I could base the class on the conversation I had with Kate, Nathan and Jake the night of Brad's funeral. But there was so much I wanted to teach, I asked spirit for assistance. And then it occurred to me to start the first class with the basics about the clairs, defining the difference between a psychic and a medium, and explaining evidential mediumship. And I wanted to include tangible activities for the attendees, for I have gotten more out of the workshops I've attended that were interactive. So while I had been reluctant at first to Megan's plans, I now found the idea exciting. I'd be teaching my students how to develop their own Gifts and strengthen their intuition even if they had no interest in becoming a professional medium.

As I typed up an outline and filled in some of the details, the familiar sound of the wind chimes pealed out over the front door. I glanced at my clock as Megan's footsteps approached my office door. She peeked in and said, "Your appointment is here."

"Okay, I'll be right there." I closed my desk, then took a few minutes to meditate and thanked spirit in advance for assisting me. I sensed that someone from spirit was already here, eager to give his message to my client.

Out at the storefront I greeted the man waiting for me at the front counter. "Hello," I said, "you must be Roger Royce."

"Yes, but you can call me Red," he said as I shook his calloused hand. He appeared to be in his mid-thirties with reddish blonde hair, a red mustache and beard. He wore wire-rimmed glasses, a black checked shirt over his broad shoulders, blue jeans and brown work boots. "I've never done this before," he said with a nervous laugh.

I smiled at him. "It'll be fine. Come with me." He followed me to my office, and we sat at the reading table. "Just a minute," I said, and closed my eyes to connect to spirit. When I opened my eyes I saw that the spirit man who had been waiting for the reading had moved behind Red's chair. "I have someone here in spirit with us. He stands behind you, showing me he is your father," I said.

Red nodded.

"Your father is holding a saw and a hammer. He was a carpenter or a builder?"

"He was both. We build cabinets and remodel houses," Red said.

I felt a stab of pain in my chest. It was so painful it brought tears to my eyes. I telepathically asked spirit about it and heard, "Cancer".

"Your father died of cancer," I said, then received more information and said, "Lung cancer."

"Yes, Ma'am, that's right."

"Your father was a smoker."

"Yes, he was. He quit when he learned he had cancer, but it was too late."

I nodded as the pain abated and took a deep breath. A scene appeared before me of Red and his father hanging cabinets on a kitchen wall. "You and your father not only worked together, you were good friends."

"Yes, Ma'am," Red said, and nodded.

"You could tell your father anything. His death was quite a shock to you on both a personal and business level."

"Yes, that's right."

"Your father says, 'Tell her I'm okay.'"

"You must mean his wife Gwen. She can't stop crying. I don't know what to do for her."

I looked at him, "His wife is not your mother."

"No, my parents divorced when I was young. My father raised me. He and Gwen married a year ago. They were happy, the happiest I can remember him ever being."

Red's father nodded that this was true, then showed me a new scene of Red with two young boys. "You have two sons?"

"Yes, Ma'am."

A new scene showed of a campground, and I said, "Your father says that life can surprise you. He says it's important to take time with your family and wishes he had done more fun things with you and his grandsons. Don't make the same mistake. Take your sons and wife camping, and sometimes take just the boys. Start a new tradition, perhaps in the fall, where you camp every year with them."

Red nodded.

"He says to tell them about nature. Tell them the stories he told you when you were young. Create a special time with just them. Teach them to fish, hunt and tie rope knots, and other things. And cook camping meals like stew or chili. Make that a part of the tradition, too. Do this each year, and continue the tradition with them and their children."

"Okay," Red said. "Would you tell Dad I miss him?"

"He knows you do, and he watches over you, your family and his wife. He says to tell Gwen that he watches over her. Tell her that he knows it's difficult, but there is more for her to do in this lifetime. He asks that you keep her a part of your family even if she remarries."

"I will."

I saw a red rose and said, "She's especially raw because their romance was still so new, so fresh. The bloom was still on the rose, so to speak. She may think her life is over, but at fifty she's not as old as she thinks. There will be another romance for her in the years ahead," I said, then blushed at the thought of Jake.

As I pushed thoughts of Jake aside, I said, "Gwen's in such emotional pain she may not listen to your words. Tell her anyway. Tell her to take it one day at a time."

A journal flashed before my eyes. "She can write to your dad each night in her journal, telling him about her day and of things for which she is grateful. At first, she will write about her sorrow, but in time she will notice things that brighten her day, and she will become eager to share that with him. This will help her."

"Okay. I'll tell her, but I don't know if she's open to any of this."

"Tell her anyway. A part of her will accept the message. The journal is a good idea for you, too. Talk to your dad in it. Get your fears and worries on paper so you can step back and see them in a new light. Kind of like the way you told him about your life when you worked side by side, only now you're writing to him."

"Okay. So am I okay?"

His question referred to his own mortality. "I see you with your grandchildren, that much I can tell you."

Red looked relieved. "I was afraid of leaving my wife and kids alone."

"But you don't smoke."

"No, Ma'am, never even tried it."

"That's good."

"What about the business? Do I have to provide for Gwen?"

"Did she work in the business with you and your father?"

"No, she's a dental hygienist, works for a dentist in town."

"I sense no conflict between you and Gwen. Did your father have a will?"

"Yes, he did."

"Did he provide for his wife in the document?."

"Yes, Ma'am."

"He's showing me a paper. It's an insurance policy and Gwen is the beneficiary."

"Yes, that's right. My lawyer made me aware of that."

"Your father is saying he bought the policy to take care of her. And in his will he stated the business was all yours."

"Yes, he did."

"So why do you feel obligated? I don't sense you owe Gwen anything, so don't look for trouble."

"That's a relief. I was also wondering about my father's share of the work. I can't keep doing it all alone."

His father's spirit showed me a new scene. "Your father is showing me that someone will be working with you. Don't make him your partner. But the man will be reliable and you can trust him."

"Who is it?"

"He will be a friend of a friend, so ask your friends if they know of a reliable carpenter that can work for you. His name begins with a D. David? Daniel? Something like that. Your father says that in the coming years, one of your sons could become your new partner."

Red smiled for the first time. "That must be my son Stewart. He loves coming to work with me already. He's only seven years old, but wants to do everything I do. I keep him busy hammering nails."

"There you go!"

Red's father smiled, then faded from view.

"Your father's gone now, but call on him if you need him. But I sense you're doing fine. Listen to your inner guidance; it's there for you, for all of us."

"Thank you."

"I'm happy to be of service."

I escorted Red to the front counter. As he paid Megan for the reading, he put several of my business cards in his pocket.

# CHAPTER FORTY-TWO

AFTER MY READING with Red, I went into my apartment in search of a snack and grabbed a bag of almonds. I popped a few into my mouth as I walked back to my office. Being with spirit often made me hungry and lately craving nuts. As I took a seat at my desk, the front door's chimes rang out and I heard Megan say, "Jennie will be with you in a minute."

I looked at my clock. I wasn't expecting anyone until later this afternoon, my last appointment of this year. With Christmas just a week away I needed to get busy buying gifts and making plans and had little time for readings.

Megan stepped into my office and said, "A man wishes to see you. He doesn't have an appointment."

"Okay," I said, then finished chewing the almonds, and sipped my bottled water. I followed her to the waiting area and greeted the gentleman seated there. "Hi, I'm Jennie. May I help you?"

"I hope so," he said as he stood from the chair.

I led him to my office, and we sat at the table. "Okay, now Mr..."

"Fred Thompson, and I need you to find something."

"Well, I'll try," I said, and closed my eyes to connect with spirit. When I opened my eyes the spirit of a Native American woman was smiling at me. She brought about a scene where she was walking in thick and lush forest, alongside a deer.

When I told Fred what I saw he said, "I don't know a thing about that."

"She is one of your guides," I said as I telepathically asked her for more information. "She walks out of the woods and stands by a lake. The deer is sipping water from the lake."

He stared at me without comment.

What was this about? He didn't seem to have a clue.

'Was this a new symbol?' I silently asked the spirit.

She pointed at the lake with emphasis, and I said, "The woman is pointing at the lake. The deer is standing near her at the water's edge. This means nothing to you?"

"A deer, an Indian woman and a lake?" He shook his head, then scratched his chin as he thought. He snapped his fingers and said, "I grew up near Dearborn, Michigan. Is that what you're talking about?"

I didn't know what I was talking about. My confidence shaken, I took a deep breath and tried to stop thinking so much as I reconnected with spirit and asked for assistance.

The spirit smiled at me as I silently asked her to show me more. "She is now back in the woods and looking at the ground," I said. "She is kicking away leaves and pointing at the soil."

He stared at me, looking confused.

I asked Mica for help, and said, "This is something your wife lost. You are not searching for something you lost?"

"Yes, that's right," he said.

"What you are looking for was lost outside." The spirit nodded and held up a key ring. "Are you looking for keys?"

"Yes, that's right," he said with a laugh. "Wow, you are good! We have been searching for the keys to our safe deposit box. My wife can't remember when she last had them."

"From seeing the leaves on the ground, I'd say the keys were lost some time ago."

The man snapped his fingers again, and said, "You know, I bet she lost them Labor Day weekend. That's when we took a trip to Deer Lake. We stopped at our bank on our way out of town."

"Did you just say Deer Lake?"

"Yeah, Deer Lake State Park, up in the Panhandle. Oh I remember now, my wife must have had the keys on her when we went there. I'll call and ask the park ranger if they found them."

I shook my head and laughed. "A deer, a lake, and keys on the ground. The spirit has answered your question," I said.

"Hey, you are right and that's amazing! We've looked everywhere, and someone suggested we ask a psychic for help. Wait till my wife hears about this."

"Yes, spirit sure is amazing," I said as the spirit and her scene faded and another one started. In this new vision a man paced back and forth holding a ruler. He looked like a teacher, maybe a professor. "Are you going to college?" I asked Fred.

He looked surprised. "Yes, I am. How could you know that?"

I didn't answer him as I watched the teacher toss a book into the trash, then retrieve it and hold it to his chest. He did this several times. What on earth was this about? Then he pointed at a chart on the wall. I decided to just give what I got. "I see a teacher tossing a book into a trash can. Then he holds the book as he points at a chart or a map on a wall."

The man laughed. "Well, isn't that something. I've recently changed my major, and I guess that's what you're talking about. I've been feeling like I've wasted time and money on the other course and books."

So this was another new symbol. The wall map must mean a new course or change of direction. As the spirit spoke I repeated, "He says it wasn't a waste of time. You will put that knowledge to good use even though you've changed your major. There was a purpose to going to that class, for the information you will need. You know the saying, don't throw the baby out with the bath water?"

"Yes," he said with a nod.

"Well, in your case it's, don't toss all that knowledge into the trash can. There's value in what you learned. Keep it, you will apply it."

He laughed. "That makes more sense than you can imagine. Thanks!"

I was glad it made sense to him; because this had been the oddest reading I've ever given.

# CHAPTER FORTY-THREE

I WAS TYPING my notes from the Red Royce and Fred Thompson readings when Megan came to my door and said, "JD is here, and has no appointment either."

I followed Megan out to the storefront, and said, "Hi, JD, what's up?"

"Are you busy?"

"Never too busy to see you, come with me."

JD followed me to my office. I closed the door, and we sat at the table.

"How are you doing? Has your memory improved? Did you go to a therapist?"

"Oh, yes, my doctor prescribed a nutritional therapy. And he referred me to a therapist who has helped me using regression therapy. I'm much happier now."

"Well, that's wonderful news! Is that what brought you here today?"

"No, and I'd rather not say. I hoped you'd tell me."

"Okay," I said. I closed my eyes, connected to spirit and as I opened my eyes saw my first client, JD's Uncle Carl smiling at me.

"Hello Miss Jennie," he said. "It was a bit tricky, but I made it here to say hello to you!"

I looked over at JD who was smiling at me. "You see him, don't you Jennie? My Uncle Carl?"

"Yes, I do. When did he pass?"

"A few weeks ago. During my dreams last night he visited me and asked me to come see you."

"Well, this is a first for me," I said. "I've never seen one of my clients on the other side of the veil before; how interesting."

Carl was smiling as another spirit appeared next to him. She held his hand, and they were both now smiling at me. "Your uncle is with his wife, your Aunt Myrtle," I said.

JD smiled. "Oh, I'm so happy to hear that. They were so in love. I am so glad he is with her."

Carl nodded, and gave me a message for JD. "Carl wants to tell you something," I said.

"What is it?"

"He says he and Myrtle were very much in love. He is showing me love as a glowing pulse of energy, and I can feel the energy vibrating in my chest!" It was so fascinating. I wanted to linger and ponder it, but needed to finish JD's message. "Carl is saying that the loving relationship you have always desired is available to you. But you first need to raise your energy level to attract it. He is now showing me a hand pump, and says, 'You need to prime the pump by loving yourself first.'"

JD blushed.

"He says to let go of the past and forgive yourself and others. Release resentment and attachment. Find things you can appreciate about them, but at least bless them and let them go. Then find things you can appreciate about yourself. Thank your hands for the ability to hug your grandchildren. Thank your feet and legs for taking you places. Thank your mouth for tasting good food. Thank your ears for listening to great music. Thank your mind for thinking wonderful thoughts, and so on. Take on an attitude of gratitude.

"From that higher plateau, love yourself. The level of love you generate within is what you give to others. And this love grows, multiplies and expands. The love you feel within is expressed from your eyes, your smile, your laughter, and your voice. Become more conscious of being loving. Stop chasing after love and instead be the love. As you become and express love more, you will shift to an even higher level. This will happen gradually and naturally as you live from gratitude, appreciation and grace.

"When you are living from this level of love, you will meet that special someone who is also seeking you. He will meet you at that higher level of being. When you meet him, you will know, because you will feel it, like Carl felt toward Myrtle. Trust it, believe it and know that level of love is attainable."

JD looked surprised. "Is he saying there's romance in my future?"

I laughed. "That's what it sounds like."

"Well, who is he? When will I meet him?"

"From Carl's message, it sounds like all will be answered in time, but that's up to you."

Carl nodded, then he and Myrtle faded from view. "He's gone now, JD."

JD smiled and said, "Thank you, Jennie. I sure didn't expect that message. I was just hoping you'd see Uncle Carl. But I do like his message, and I'll take it."

She hugged me, and said, "You know, people have the wrong idea about mediums. I'm sure there are charlatans and scam artists out there... heck, Uncle Carl met a few of them over the years. But mediums that use their Gifts as you do are to be appreciated."

"Thank you, JD, but it is spirit who is so wise and wonderful. I'm just the instrument, a transceiver for their messages of love and healing."

☼

As I escorted JD to the front door my cellphone rang. I pulled it from my pocket and saw from the caller ID that it was my son. "I need to take this, JD. Have a wonderful holiday and New Years."

"You too, Jennie," she said, and waved goodbye as she left the store.

"Hi, Nathan," I said as I answered the phone.

"Hi, Mom. I called to give you our flight information."

"Just a minute, let me walk back to my office," I said as I rushed down the hallway. Seated at my desk, I said, "Okay, what is it?"

"We'll be landing in Orlando at 3:30."

"That's on Thursday, right?"

"Yes, Christmas Eve," he said, then gave me the name of the airline and the flight number. "I hope Bridgette does okay."

"Why? Does she tend to get airsick?"

He was quiet a beat, then said, "Oops. We wanted to tell you together."

"Tell me what?"

"We're expecting!"

"Oh, that's wonderful news! Is Bridgette feeling up to travel?"

"The doctor says she'll be okay, and we really want to be there with all of you."

"Does she need me to buy anything special for her eat or drink?"

"Just have a box of crackers on hand. Other than that, she's craving ice cream."

"What flavor?"

"Any as long as it contains peanut butter and chocolate chunks."

I added ice cream and crackers to my ever growing shopping list as I hung up the phone. While I felt elated at having another grandchild to love in just a few months, that elation soon turned to overwhelm. There was so much to do before the holidays... planning, shopping, baking! I wanted everything to be perfect, and that included the comfort of my now pregnant daughter-in-law while she, Nathan and Emily stayed with me in my apartment. And on top of all that there was the workshop for January.

My cell phone rang again.

"Hi Jake," I said.

"Hey, Jennie, I've been thinking."

"Oh? What about?"

"Since your family will all be together for the holidays, why wait? Let's get married on New Year's Eve."

I nearly dropped the phone.

# JENNIE'S STORY CONTINUES

### Book 2: Dancing on Moonbeams
Jennie's paranormal abilities expand and unfold even more as she communicates with the spiritual realms, delivering messages to her clients. And one out of body experience is so pleasurable that the psychic medium doesn't want to come back from it! But all is not delightful. Jennie's ex-husband and his mother still push her buttons. Why won't they just leave her alone? And while ghostly apparitions are the norm by day, the spirits have taken to invading her dreams. What do they want to tell her as she strolls the moonbeam streams?

### Book 3: Finding Faith
While on vacation, Jennie's best friend and fellow medium, Deanna, asks her to go to North Carolina in her place to help in finding a missing coed. Jennie is reluctant. Not only is she enjoying her time off... she's never tried to find a missing person. But when Jennie discovers that she knew the missing girl's parents years ago, she agrees she must help. Her quest takes her deep inside the world of dreams, searching for clues as she travels with astral friends; and riding horseback and all-terrain vehicles. But will all this adventure help her succeed at Finding Faith?

### Author's Books Page
www.amazon.com/Lynn-Thomas/e/B001K8U8BW
www.amazon.co.uk/Lynn-Thomas/e/B001K8U8BW

# About the Author

Lynn Thomas discovered her joy for writing while in childhood alongside her grandmother and mother as they spun stories, poems and songs. Lynn loves going to the beach, playing golf with her husband, eating chocolate, and contemplating metaphysics and the esoteric. And in addition to time spent with her family, her passion is creating inspirational entertainment for her readers.

## A Note From Lynn Thomas

Thank you so much for reading *Jennie's Gifts Book One*. If you enjoyed it, please take a moment to leave a review at your favorite online retailers, such as Amazon US or Amazon UK.

And I welcome contact from readers, so please visit my website to email me, sign up for the free newsletter to receive updates on new releases and special offers, read the blog, and find links for social networking. I look forward to hearing from you!

www.LynnThomas.info

– Lynn Thomas